750 PENNY DREADFUL.—Buntline (Ned)
The King of the Sea : a tale of the fearless
and free, *illustrated*, 1848—Hazel (Harry)
The Corsair, or the foundling of the sea :
a romance, *illustrated*, N.D.—2 vols in one,
8vo. old half morocco, *stained*, 7s 6d

THE KING OF THE SEA.

THE

KING OF THE SEA.

A TALE OF THE FEARLESS AND FREE.

BY NED BUNTLINE.

"The waves were white, and red the morn,
In the noisy hour when I was born;
And the whale it whistled, and the porpoise rolled,
And the dolphins bared their backs of gold;
And never was heard such an outcry wild
As welcomed to life the OCEAN CHILD."

LONDON:
PUBLISHED BY GEO. PEIRCE, 310, STRAND.
1848.

LONDON:
PRINTED BY GEORGE PEIRCE, 310, STRAND.

THE KING OF THE SEA.

CHAPTER I.

"The waves were white, and red the morn
In the noisy hour when I was born;
And the whale it whistled, the porpoise rolled,
And the dolphins bared their backs of gold,
And never was heard such an outcry wild
As welcomed to life the *Ocean-child!*"

A WILD and fearful night was that which followed the twentieth day of March, in the year 1822. On this night, upon the heaving bosom of the broad Atlantic ocean, the packet ship Prescott, from London, bound to Boston, was hove to under her close-reefed storm-sails. The gale, a heavy northwester, was too violent for her to hold on her course, and there she lay, pitching and heaving like a drunken soldier over a rough pavement, with all her light spars housed, and but a scant show of canvass spread to the wind.

Her commander (a true-hearted, weather-beaten son of Neptune was that same Captain Jack Bowline), was standing close alongside of the helmsman, with his speaking trumpet in hand, watching the heavy rollers as they swept down upon his quivering ship, and giving from time to time, in a quick low tone, his orders to the helmsman, as the storm-tossed bark came up or fell off under the heavy surge of the sea and the force of the gale. The officers of the ship and the crew were all on deck, attending to their numerous duties; keeping a bright look-out on their preventer-braces and stays, and standing by to reduce even the scanty sail which was set, if it was necessary. It was indeed a fearful night. The sea rolled wild and dark around, the scud flew whistling through the

(1)

rigging, the ship groaned and creaked like some living thing in pain, as she staggered through the heaving waters.

But one person beside the crew and officers could be seen upon the deck, and he was ————, not the KING OF THE SEA, but one who deserves the reader's attention, because he will hereafter hold a conspicuous station in this history. He was striding hastily to and fro along the quarter-deck, as if his mind was wrought up into a strange state of excitement, although he did not seem to fear the storm or note its fury; his eye was downcast, his brow pale, and his lips closed, as if to keep back the expression of agony which spoke in his looks.

The firm, quick step of this person denoted youth, strength, and activity; his figure, although it was enveloped in a large sea-cloak, seemed tall and noble; his carriage was majestic, and as each turn in his walk brought him alongside the binnacle lamp, its light fell upon his face, a face which once seen could never be forgotten.

A high and broad forehead of marble pallor was overhung with thick masses of dark brown hair; his eyes of dark blue, were shadowed by heavy shaggy brows; his lip was thin, and at either extremity drawn down into a curve expressive of deep and firm determination. His whole face was indicative of a proud and haughty disposition. He seemed a being born to command, with a full comprehension of his birthright, yet without the power to insure its dues; for his face was marked with the furrows of care and vexation.

There was a wild and restless anxiety in his every motion as he strode along the deck. Every now and then he would pause as he reached the companion way which led down to the cabin, then listen for a moment and clasp his hands together with an expression of agony, as the sounds of feeble moans from some suffering being below would come up faintly to his ears.

Of all who were on deck, he alone seemed heedless of the storm. The crew and officers, with anxious hearts, were contemplating the dangers of the raging hurricane; but *he* cast no look upon the strained and bending spars; his glance fell not upon the waters which were heaving around him like snow-capped mountains tossed and shook by an earthquake.

"Mr. Edmiston takes his poor wife's sickness right hard, Captain Bowline," said the man at the helm, to the old skipper, who stood beside him.

"Ay, that he does," said the old man, "and I don't much wonder at it! The poor sweet creature has been used to better times, and the sea, in a blow like this, is a fearful place for a young thing like her to be taken down on. But it will soon be over in some way or other!"

Still strode the stranger whom they called Edmiston, up and down the spray-washed deck, and yet his face wore its look of deep anxiety. More often did he pause by the companion way now, for louder and more frequent came the moans which seemed to agonise his heart.

"Oh God!" said he, in a deep tone of suffering, "Oh God, why cannot I be by her side? They say it is better for her not to see me, but oh, 'tis hard to hear her moans and know that I cannot help, or even console her with my presence!"

At this moment a piercing scream was heard from the cabin, and again and again was it repeated. Its effect seemed maddening to him. With a bound, as if he sprang to grasp some giant foe, he gained the hatchway; another step and he was at the cabin door. Loud and hastily he drove his clenched hand against the door of the cabin, from which the sounds of agony came.

"Judith! Judith, open the door! I can stay away no longer; Oh, God, I cannot bear *this!*" cried he, as the fearful screams still continued. But the door was fastened, no answer came to his appeal. More angry was his tone as again he shouted, "Open the door, you black wench! Open, before I burst it from its hinges!"

"Jis wait and keep cool another minnit, massa! Missis be better soon;" answered a voice from within. And then the shrieks became more and more faint, and soon all was still.

"Oh! God, she is dead! she is dead!" said he, as he listened in vain for the sounds he had heard. In his desperation he was on the point of attempting to burst in the door, when it opened and the curly head of a negress was thrust out.

"It's all well now, massa; missy get better now; you may come in purty soon after directly!"

"Don't deceive me, wench! Is she not dead?"

"Ki! massa; no, I tell you just fore now she was git better, and she's got two of de lubliest—"

He waited not for any further information, but dashed her aside and rushed into the cabin.

"Ki! I guess my massa hab run mad!" said the negress, as she picked herself up from the deck, where she had fallen when he pushed her out of the way.

"What's the matter? What are you about there on your beam-ends, snow-ball?" said one of the crew, as he stepped forward in true sailorlike gallantry to help the Ethiopian damsel to her feet.

"None o' your imprence, Mistaw Sailaw!" cried she, indignantly; "I don't look like none o' your beams's ends, nor no snow-ball nuther! I jist thank you to hoe your own row and let dis child alone *now!*"

"Why, you needn't git into no tantrums, you half-washed she-dragon, you. I wasn't agoing to kiss your big blubber lips!"

"Sah!" screamed she, now thoroughly maddened by his taunts, "Sah, I wont be indignified dis ere way no more! *No, Sah!* I go tell your captain, an' if *he* don't gib you goss, *I* will!"

Away she staggered across the deck of the heaving vessel, to lay her complaint before the Captain. As he saw her coming, with a smile upon his face, he spoke :—

"Well, Miss Judith!" said he, "I'm glad to see you on deck again; I hope all's well below?"

She forgot her wrongs in a moment, being now so politely addressed by the Captain, and while her mouth opened into a six-inch grin, she answered—

"Oh, yes, Massa Cap'n, it's all right now, only you got two more passengers dan you had dis morning; dat's all!"

"*Two*, Judith?"

"Yes, Massa Cap'n; a lily boy an' a wee young lady as will be if she grow up!"

"Well, I'm glad to hear it, but it is dangerous for you to stay up here on deck! If one of them seas happen to come aboard, it will wash you away!"

"Tank you, massa, I tink I go down stairs den; it wouldn't do for me to be loss overboard now, nohow, case Ize got de babies to nuss, bress dear little possum hearts!—I lubs 'em a'ready."

With the last expression she disappeared down the cabin hatch-way, her movements having been considerably accelerated by being tripped up with a rope, which the sailor who had made her so angry, had stretched across the cabin door close to the deck. She did not hurt herself by the fall, however, as she fortunately struck *head* first.

"I pity them ere two youngsters, Cap'n Bowline, I do!" said the helmsman, evidently alluding to those who had just been ushered into existence.

"Why so, Ned? They are not so much to be pitied, with a *man* for a father, and a sweet kind woman for a mother; and then, I reckon that Mr. Edmiston has ballast enough to keep them in trim!"

"It isn't that, Cap'n, that I'm considerin' on; they may have good parents and lots o' chink, and all that, but I never seed a March born child that didn't have lots of trouble! It seems as if their lives are always as stormy as the month they're born in."

"Well, I never did think of that before!" said Captain B—., "but I do believe it's a *fact*, for my cousin Ned was born on a March morning, and that boy has seen almost every thing but the devil himself! He's been knocked into a cocked hat a hundred times, and there aint an inch of him left that isn't writ over with some mark of the hard knocks that have been hove into him at one time or another!"

"Yes, sir, it *is* a fact, for I've know'd more cases than I could spin off in a midwatch yarn; but there's one thing sartin—the boys that are born in March, always turn out to be *men;* I never know'd a milk-sop or a spooney, as was born in March. They have lots of trouble, but they stand up to it like men, and that's half the battle, you know!"

"Ay, and the best half at that! I wish the half of this nor'-wester was over. Look out there! let her come up a little and ease her off into the trough as the rolls pass! This is heavy weather, but the old ship acts like herself in it. Ah! there comes a streak of day to leeward. I wouldn't wonder if the clouds broke away by the looks there to east'ard!"

"Don't know, sir!" said the helmsman, "but I thinks it looks a little serspishus yet, as the old woman said of the snake-skin after it was dried and stuffed! I hope it'll hold up, but these ere nor'westers are as long-winded as a Tennessee parson that's preaching a trial sermon for a *call*."

The colloquy was ended by the sudden appearance on deck of him whom we described in the first part of this chapter—Mr. Edmiston. His countenance was so altered that one who had seen him an hour before, would now have scarcely recognised him. It was radiant with joy; flushed with pleasure.

"Give me joy, Captain Bowline!" said he; "I am a *father*, and my dear wife is, I hope, out of danger."

"I do from my heart, sir!" said the Captain, "for I pitied your misery awhile ago, when you were stamping up and down the deck, as much as if I'd been in your place."

"Thank you! thank you! There is nothing which will touch the heart quicker than sympathy. I was, indeed, a sufferer, but my present joy repays all. Do you think this gale will last much longer?"

"No, I've an idea by the way the day breaks there through the ragged clouds in the east, that we've had the heaviest of it. I hope so, for this losing time works cross-grained with the owners. They're always counting hours when a ship is on expenses."

"Where are we now?"

"Why, we're about midway of the passage. A good breeze would run us in within eight or nine days. But it's always tarnal thick on the banks at this season, and the sails and rigging are too stiff in the cold to work well, so that it may take us a little longer. —Ah! look out there, Mr. Edmiston! steady yourself; if that roller breaks aboard it'll make a clean sweep!"

The huge wave which he saw rolled down and struck the ship just abaft the main shrouds; it seemed as if it would sweep bulwarks and all with it.

"Hold on hard for your lives!" shouted the Captain, as he saw it coming down—and each one grasped to the shrouds and tackling. Edmiston, with a light bound seized a backstay, and swung himself up into the mizen shrouds, escaping even the spray, which for a moment had hidden the deck from his view. The sea did no serious damage, and though it completely flooded the deck, it soon ran off through the lee scuppers.

"Why, Mr. Edmiston, you can dodge a sea better than an old sailor!" said the Captain, as he wiped the salt water from about his eyes and face. "By the way you keep your legs and use yourself aboard, I'd think you were an old salt. If you hadn't shore toggery on, I'm sure I'd hail ye for an old cruiser, by the very cut of your jib."

"Well, Captain, you wouldn't be far wrong!" answered the other. "This isn't the first time I've trod a deck, nor is this the first gale that I've listened to."

"Well, sir, I had a kind of an idea that way; but you didn't say nothing about it, and so I thought I'd missed my reckoning. May I ask in what service you've cruised, for I know you're a man-o'-war's-man?"

"I've served His Majesty, the King of Great Britain, for twenty years; but, thank God, I'm free from him and tyranny now! I see you have a curiosity to know something of me, Captain Bowline, and as my dear little wife is sleeping now, I'll take time enough to spin you a short yarn. You know my name. I am the youngest son of Sir Launcelot Edmiston, who placed me in the navy as a midshipman, when I was fourteen years of age; I was fortunate in seeing service, was promoted, and one year ago was in command of as fine a frigate as ever floated—the Leander. But at that time I married, as my *noble* father thought, one whose blood was not so good as mine; in this I incurred his displeasure. I ventured to remonstrate with him against his ill treatment, and for this not only lost his patronage with the government, but was disinherited. My command was taken from me through his influence and given to young Lord Hawkhurst, who has scarcely seen as many months' sea-service as I have served years. One week before you sailed' this same puppy, Captain Lord Hawkhurst, insulted my wife, that angel who now sleeps in your cabin, whom he had before pestered with his insolent attentions. I challenged him, we met, and I have *only* wounded the wretch, whom I should have *killed!* I knew that I should be prosecuted, and to avoid the injustice and disgrace of a court-martial, I resigned my commission. I have taken passage in your ship, and now you know all. I am on my way to a land of free men, where there are no lords save the Lord God of Heaven; where there are no tyrants, and no *titles* to descend to an *elder* son. Why, sir, I have been spurned by my own brother from my father's door; but now, all ties are cut adrift; with my wife and her sweet babies I will shape a new course o'er the ocean of life. Henceforth I am an *American!*"

"You are a trump anyhow, and the highest in the pack," said Captain Bowline, as he warmly grasped the speaker's hand. The bright tears raised in his eyes as he continued: "You shall never lack a father or brother, or want a shot in your locker, while Jack Bowline sails, and there's my fist on it—but I do wish you had used up that infernal Lord Hoghurst (you called him, didn't you? but darn his name), you ought to have clewed up and furled his canvass!"

"We may meet again," said Edmiston; and then as he grasped the noble old skipper's hard hand, he continued: "I thank you,

Captain Bowline, for your good feeling. If I can ever lend you a hand in any way, you know where to call for it. But see! The sun is breaking out! I think the wind will go down as he rises! I must go down now and see how my poor wife fares!"

"There goes one of God's noblemen; one that would have been a man if he had been born in a kitchen, who needs no assistance but his own heart and free mind to attain his right position in a free world!" said Bowline, as the form of his passenger disappeared down the companion-way. "But I do wish to goodness he had used up the puppy that insulted his sweet young wife. I wonder what he'll turn to doing, when he gets into port? I must find out how he's off for tin, and mayhap I can lend him a hand in the start-off!"

"I think Mr. Edmiston was about three-thirds right, Cap'n Bowline, when he said this ere blow had run itself about out o'breath!" said Ned Brace, the helmsman.

"Ay, that he was; if it lulls down this way long, we'll soon have the canvass on her again. I guess we can let one watch turn in now, and get a little snooze; the poor fellows have had a long spell on deck. You've had that wheel in hand ten hours, haven't you?"

"A matter of summat that, or more; but that's nothin' to me, when its all hands."

"Well, all hands have done their duty, and so has the old craft, and one more blow is weathered!" said the old Captain; then hailing his chief mate, he continued: "Mr. Cringle, you may let the larboard watch turn in, and get your dreaming tacks aboard, yourself! The worst of the blow is over, and I guess the starboard watch and me can take care of the barkie now. Send a man here to relieve Ned Brace at the helm!"

"Ay, ay, sir!" was the cheerful answer.

CHAPTER II.

Revenge! revenge! is still the cry,
  More sweet than music to my ear!
Revenge! revenge! and he must die,
  Who dared athwart my course to steer.

ON a couch hung around with rich curtains of crimson velvet, a couch of downy softness, lay a young man whose deadly pallor betokened extreme illness. Hair as dark and glossy as the wing of the spotless raven, and eyes of intense blackness aided to contrast with his singular paleness. His lips too were bloodless, and ever and anon a spasmodic quiver would betoken the agony which he seemed to suffer.

By his bedside stood a young and elegantly-dressed man; around the room were servants in livery, waiting the commands of their service. The room was fitted out with elegant and costly furniture, betokening the opulence of its occupants.

"Are you in much pain, Hawkhurst?" asked the person who stood beside the couch of him who lay thereon.

"*Pain!* Yes, the pains of hell couldn't be worse than the agony of this shattered thigh of mine, and the worst of *all* is that he, my rival in love, my enemy in all things, has gone off without a scratch! Have you heard what has become of him?"

"Yes! he has gone to America; first resigning his commission!"

"And his *wife?*"

"Has gone with him, of course! Do you think he would leave her here for you to make love to?"

"Hell and fury! Has *she* and he both escaped me? *Escaped!* said I? No! no! not while we three live! Roxanna Eldon refused my proferred love and gave a heart and hand to my sworn foe! Roxanna Edmiston scorned and reviled a passion which her own beauty had driven on even to madness! Her husband has added yet another to all these damning insults, and shall they pass *unavenged?* No; by the soul of my father, I will *live* but for *revenge!* I will make that proud, beautiful woman sue for my favour! I will teach her to know what scorn, and insult, and wrong are!"

"Be calm, my friend, this excitement will retard your recovery."

"Be *calm?* Go bid the mad ocean be calm while the wild hurricane careers over its rushing waters; go chain the red lightnings of high heaven; go curb and dam up the boiling lava which rolls down Etna's rocky sides! but do not try to stay the course of *my* revenge."

"How can you reach him or her? They are beyond your reach."

"Beyond my reach? Are they beyond the frozen poles of the earth? Are they where mortal may not breathe, and live, and move? Have not I wealth, power, a soul to dare, a mind to plan, and a hand to execute all that man *dare* plan? You know me not, James Clare, if you think that common obstacles can thwart me! Time, space, all things will I overcome, but I never will rest, till I have triumphed over him who has cast me on this couch of suffering, over her who has scorned and thwarted my dreams of love! Yes, I loved her, she the poor daughter of a broken down gentleman, and I the oldest son and heir of one of England's noblest and wealthiest peers; I loved her! But the love which was strong is turned into hate, and the depth of my wrong has written her fate! She shall yet be mine!"

"You are certainly very bitter, Hawkhurst; but all I can say is—success to you. You know I've stood by you in the whole of this affair."

"Yes, Clare, you have, like a noble friend, and I appreciate your friendship. I shall not soon forget it; but I feel very faint—this excitement has been overmuch for me, I fear; I wish you'd send a servant out for the doctor again."

The request was instantly complied with, and in a moment a dapper little old man, with small gray eyes and an exceedingly red nose, his thin form neatly dressed in black, stood by the side of the invalid.

"Ah, my lord, you have been talking again!" said he, as he felt the feverish pulse of the invalid. "If this excitement is kept up, we cannot with any degree of scientific precision calculate the amount

(2)

of injury which it will most undoubtedly and inevitably produce. We must insist upon your preserving a tranquil and serene state and disposition of mind and body, until the change which our prescriptions will cause is fully apparent."

"How long will it be before I can get up from this infernal bed, doctor? Just tell me in plain English. Now, I don't want any of your long hum-drum essays!" exclaimed the patient, impatiently.

"I always speak pure English, my lord," said the doctor, with an air of insulted dignity.

"That's no answer to my question, sir!" returned the invalid. "Just let me know how soon you can cure me; or if you can't tell, perhaps Doctor Pillgarlic, if sent for—"

"It will be quite unnecessary to send for him, my lord! If the bone knits well, in about forty days from the present, your lordship may expect to be able to take gentle exercise, that is with the aid of our undivided and most scientific care and attention. But, sir, do not speak of Doctor Pillgarlic—he never could have extracted that ball from your thigh, and have so arranged and splintered the broken bone as we have. He has only graduated at three colleges, and we have diplomas from seven!"

"Forty days more of this infernal inactivity? By heaven, it is worse than death! But it can't be avoided, and there's no use of grumbling. You may leave me, sir. I prefer the company of my friend, Mr. Clare."

"Certainly, my lord; but permit us to recommend calmness, and an extensive proportion of serene composure. We think it advisable that you do not imbibe more than three diminutive glasses of port per day, and we—"

"Oh, go to the devil and leave me in quietness, will you?" cried the invalid, thoroughly sickened with the pomposity of his medical attendant, who, although a man of whims and caprices, was still a person of decided merit in his profession.

"Certainly, my lord, your wish shall be obeyed," answered the doctor; but as, with an air of mortified dignity, he left the room, he muttered, "We'll pay him off for this! He shall feel it the next time we dress his thigh! Hum-drum, eh? Go to the devil, eh? We'll make him ache for it! Our dignity shall not thus be trampled upon. He'll wish he had Doctor Pillgarlic, before we have done with him! Hum-drum, eh?"

But in these remarks the little doctor took good care not to be overheard.

"I think I can sleep now for a little while, Clare, since that old bore has gone," said Hawkhurst. "You amuse yourself as you best can, old fellow. There are books and papers to read, you'll find some of that old port, which old Gangrene wants me to take but 'three diminutive glasses per day' of, on the sideboard. You know how to make yourself at-home, my boy. Just close the curtains a bit, and let me try to get a little sleep."

It was done, the curtains were closed, and so is this chapter.

CHAPTER III.

Oh, woman! woman! in life's sky
Thou art the brightest star;
On thee alone man rests his eye
In trouble's madd'ning hour:
From thee alone to him is given
Consolation's holy balm;
With thee, earth is half a heaven—
Without thee, all a hell!

IT was fifteen days after that which opened our history in the first chapter, and the Prescott was yet at sea, although within a few hours' sail of her destined port. It was near the hour of sunset, a very light two-knot easterly breeze was barely filling the sails of the ship which were spread from every yard and spar. Oh! how different seems she now in her calm and lofty beauty, from her appearance in the fearful storm in which we saw her before, struggling in a mass of heaving, roaring, foaming waters. Now, gently gliding along over the softly rippling waves, like some beautiful and majestic woman gliding over a sunny meadow; then, in her shorn and shattered state, plunging and heaving on the dark sea, like some poor ragged maniac rushing through a forest.

Captain Bowline and Mr. Edmiston were seated on the trunk of the cabin near the taffrail in conversation, the crew were lazily scattered about the decks, the man at the helm being the only one who had anything to do, so gentle and steady was the breeze.

"What do you intend to do when you get ashore, Mr. Edmiston? How are you off for funds? Be candid and tell me, for I'm your friend in purse as in heart!" said Captain Bowline to his passenger, as they set with their eyes to landward.

"Thank you, my kind friend! I thank you more for the offer and the spirit that prompts it, than I would for the proferred assistance. But I think I shall get along. I have about four hundred pounds sterling left, and I have thought with this to settle my wife comfortably on shore in some safe and quiet place, and then to enter the merchant service, for I have no profession but that of a sailor. I think with my education and experience I can get a command."

"To be sure you can! My owners shall give you one, or else Jack Bowline won't sail in their employ another voyage. I'll see them as soon as we drop our mud-hook in Boston harbour. They've got four or five ships in the East India trade and that's a profitable business and a good chance for private ventures!"

"Yes, it is; but it would be unpleasant from the length of the voyages; it would keep me so long absent from my dear wife and her sweet babes."

"You are not speaking of absence, my husband?" said a voice

by his side; and he looked upon the form of his wife who had just come upon deck from the cabin, followed by the negress, Judith, who bore in her arms two sweet little blue-eyed cherubs.

"Ah, my Roxanna, you on deck? I fear this exertion is too much for you. Sit here by me;" and he wrapped his sea-cloak close around her tender form as he spoke.

"I was so tired of that dreary cabin!" said she. "I wanted once more to breathe fresh air, and look upon the beautiful ocean and the white sails!"

She who spoke, was indeed beautiful. She did not look to be more than seventeen; her hair of rich, dark brown, fell in soft ringlets upon her snow-white neck; her eyebrows were slightly arched over eyes of deep, liquid hazel; eyes large and soulful and full of intellectual expression. Her features were not classically regular, yet there was not one that could have been improved by alteration. Her form was slight, yet perfectly graceful, and her whole appearance beautiful, though not in the style of any model of beauty.

"Judith, bring me the children!" said Edmiston to the nurse.

"Yes, massa, I bring you de dear little posies. Massa Edward has been kickin' an' crowin' to come to you for dis long time."

"Bless the dear boy!" was the warm exclamation of the proud father, as he received the little child. "My own Roxy, I live now but in you and these sweet babes!"

"And yet you were speaking of absence from us, when I came upon deck," said she, mournfully.

"Only temporary, dearest. I have no profession save that in which I have spent my life. I cannot have you exposed to its dangers."

"Why not? Oh! my husband, there is no danger which I so much fear as your loss. If you perish, it would be far better for me to perish with you, than to endure the living death of a life of loneliness. If you still follow the sea, let me go with you! I cannot bear your absence."

"Dearest, absence would be painful to me as to yourself; but let us speak of other things now, and chase away sad thoughts. Oh! how like me this sweet babe will be. His eyes are not like thy soft and melting orbs, but there is even now a spark of the spirit's fire in them! Oh, my Edward, my ocean-born, darling boy!"

"Land ho!" shouted the look-out from aloft, at this instant; and, of course, all was excitement and joy.

"Where away?" shouted the captain.

"Dead ahead, sir! Right in the wake of the sun! The sun is setting behind it and it makes it loom up!"

"Very well! Keep a bright look-out for sails a-head, the pilot-boats will heave in sight soon!"

"Ay, ay, sir! I think there's one off the land now. I see a

speck of white to leeward, but it's in the glare of the sun, and I can't make it out plain!"

"Very well! Let me know her bearings, when the sun goes down!" "Ay, ay, sir!"

The captain now turned to Edmiston and his wife, who were still sitting on the trunk, and with great glee addressed them —

"Well, we will be in port in the morning! I want you and your wife and babies, not leaving out Judith, to go right up to my house as soon as you get ashore. You needn't make no palaver about it now, you've got to stay till you can get fixed to suit yourselves better. My Fanny has a knack of always liking those whom her husband deems worthy of his friendship, and my little Freddy and Bella will be delighted to have your sweet little youngsters to play with!"

"Noble friend, you are too good!" cried Edmiston, as he grasped the old captain's hand within his own. "The gain of one such friend as you, would repay the loss of fifty such as I have left behind me!"

"There, don't say nothing more about it!" said the honest old sailor, as he cordially returned Edmiston's grasp. "That matter's all settled; but the fog will settle soon as the sun is down. You'd better lug the babies below, and take that lily of yours out of the cold!"

Edmiston, as he was advised, removed his family into the cabin and remained there with them.

The ship stood in toward the land, Captain Bowline and his crew keeping a bright lookout for a pilot. Darkness came on, and in it we will leave them for the night.

CHAPTER VI.

Land ho! loud swells the sound,
While hearts responsive bound ;
Land ho! the joyful cry
Rings clear, and loud, and high ;
Land ho! before the blast
The good ship speeds more fast ;
Land ho! the harbour's gained,
And form to form is strained
In welcome's fond embrace ;
And on the seaman's face,
A path to tears unknown,
The tear of joy creeps down.

Oh, Heaven! it is sweet
To see a sailor meet
His wife and little weans,
Whom he has seen in dreams
So oft upon the sea,
When all uneasily
He slept amid the storm
Which howled above his form ;
From perils safe, sweet rest
He finds and deems him blest.

THE morning's sun arose, and with it a pilot came on board the Prescott, which had been hove-to between the capes during the night. All was joy on board the ship, as a fresh breeze filling all her sails alow and aloft, swept her on up the "island bay;" for there were many on board who expected to be soon clasped to the throbbing bosoms of loved ones, who had long been with them in their dreams, although absent in their waking hours.

The vessel, with her gayest streamers flying out from each mast-head like tongues of glad salutation, sped swiftly up the harbour. Fort Columbus was passed, the domes and spires of America's Athens rose in view, and soon the ready seamen sprang aloft as Captain Bowline cheerily shouted,

"Stand by to reduce sail! In with all the stu'n'-sails! clew up and furl the royals!" Soon were the light and fluttering sails bound to the yards, and then again the order: "In top-gallant-sails! Down flying jib!"

And this was quickly done, and as the courses had already been hauled up, the beautiful ship stood on up the harbour under her three topsails, jib, and spanker. More slowly, yet even more gracefully than before, she slipped along till she was abeam of that memorable spot where the Boston Indians gave King George his first Yankee tea-party, and demonstrated to the world that freemen's shoulders though broad and strong, would not bear the load of un-just taxation. Here, when she was abreast of Long Wharf, the topsails were clewed up and the jib hauled down, and then as the helm was put a-lee, the ship swerved to the wind, and rounded-to. Her headway ceased, the last order was given—

"Clear away the chain—stand by the stoppers—let go the anchor, and veer to forty fathoms!"

Then came the heavy plunge of the anchor into the water, and the rattling of the chain cable through the iron hawse-hole, and in a moment more the ship lay asleep upon the glassy bosom of the harbour. Boats from shore were soon alongside, bringing friends, consignees, &c., &c. But why should I tire the reader, for whom I have a kind and friendly feeling, with a long description of the every-day-to-be-seen arrival of a ship?

Let me transport you one half hour later, to a neat little cottage which stands between Bunker's Hill and the Navy Yard, at Charlestown, which place fronts on Boston harbour. In the neat front parlour of this cottage, behold a very *young*-looking elderly lady, with mild, dark eyes, an intellectual countenance, upon which the hand of her Maker had written the sign of amiability; a face on which care or vexation had written no wrinkle or mark. She seems a picture of happy contentment. On her right hand sits a dark-haired, black-eyed daughter, a sweet girl of fourteen or there-abouts; and upon the carpet at her feet, is a dear, rosy-cheeked little fellow of three or four years' lifetime, artlessly amusing him-self with a quantity of playthings. The daughter was reading aloud to her mother; but at the moment when we take the liberty of introducing the reader to this scene, she was interrupted by the bright-eyed youngster on the carpet.

"Ma!" said he, "ma, I do wish my papa would come home!"

"So do we all, my Freddy!" answered the mother.

"But not so much as I do, ma, because he don't give you and Bella candy like he does me. You *can't* love him as I do!"

The mother smiled, and remarked to her daughter that there was very little love in this world which was not selfish in some way or other, and then she arose with a sigh and went to the window which opened towards the bay.

"Indeed, I echo little Freddy's wish, that his dear father might come home!" sighed she. "He has had a long passage, and what with the drifting ice and easterly storms, it must be a dangerous one. But he is in the hands of God, and it is for me to hope, and pray, and trust; but not to murmur."

Why did her eyes gleam so gladly as she again glanced from the window? why did a flush of gladness light up her placid face, as the sun lights up the bosom of a clear and waveless lake in summer time?

"Oh, Freddy," she cried, "papa *is* coming! Run to meet and kiss him. You may go too, Bella. But see, he has strangers with him; I must keep my dignity tacks aboard, as he says, and wait for him here. Oh, my John, this one joy of seeing you come home well, repays all the hours of sorrow which I have passed in your absence!"

With a wild cry of gladness the two children rushed from the cottage to meet their father, whom we need not say was Captain Jack Bowline. With a bound like a young bird making its first short flight from the ground up to its mother's nest, little Freddy sprang into his father's arms; but Bella, a little abashed by the presence of strangers, only put her white arms round about his neck, and gave him a kiss as warm and pure as her own heart.

"These are my babies, Mr. Edmiston," said Bowline, as the large tears of joy chased each other down his rough and weather-bronzed cheeks.

"And whose babies are *them,* papa?" said little Fred, whose quick eyes had rested upon the ocean-born twins, which were in the arms of Judith, the negress.

"They are little dolls sent for you to play with, Freddy!" said the proud father.

"For *me,* papa? Oh, let me get down and go and kiss 'em! Who sent 'em to me? Was it cousin Ned—*my* cousin Ned?"

The party, which consisted only of the Edmiston family and Captain Bowline, walked slowly up the little green toward the house, for Mrs. Edmiston was very feeble, and yet how beautiful she looked as she leaned upon her husband's arm so trusting and confidingly. So slowly did they advance, that Mrs. Bowline, in her impatience to clasp her husband in her warm embrace of welcome, forgot her "dignity tacks," and sprang from the open door to meet him. As with a hasty step he advanced to meet her, he spoke but one word: "*Fanny!*" and yet that word spoke more love in its tone than we could describe in a page, and as their lips met, her only answer—

"*John, dear John!*" was equally expressive of her full-hearted happiness.

" Fanny," said Bowline, as soon as the first embrace was given, turning to his friends, " here's my friends, Mr. and Mrs. Edmiston, and their two little twin rose-buds, that I've brought home to pay us a visit."

With a graceful salutation, Mrs. B. at once advanced to the fair stranger, and with a sweet smile welcomed her and her husband to the cottage.

" My husband's friends are always my friends," said she.

" There, I told you that, Mr. Edmiston !" said Bowline, with an air of gratified and honourable pride. " My Fanny is a jewel, and I wouldn't swap her off for all the gems that were ever worn or dug up ! But let's go into the house; your lily is bending with fatigue. Come in, wife, and let's have a hot cup of coffee and the chicken fixens, for what with the excitement of coming into port and all that, I'm as hungry as a shark, and I reckon that the rest of us are *all same so*, as the Chinamen say. Hi yaw ! Freddy, won't you have fun with them little youngsters ?"

" Can they eat, papa ?" asked the little fellow.

" Try 'em, my boy !"

" I would, papa, only I aint got no candy to give 'em !" replied the cunning youngster, who was looking out for himself as well as for them.

" Ay, ay, got no candy, eh ? I see through you, my little monkey ! But you *shall* have some candy. Here, Bella, here's some *shiners;* take 'em and buy the youngster some candy, and buy for yourself whatever you want, my darling."

Away flew the children to make their purchases, and as Mrs. Bowline was busy in preparing a late breakfast for her husband and guests, we will listen to a conversation between Mr. Edmiston and Bowline; Mrs. E. having retired with Mrs. B. to an inner room to rest and arrange her toilet.

" You see how snug I'm fixed here, now, Mr. Edmiston," said Bowline; " and I want to have you understand that this is your house as much as it is mine, for the present !"

" I thank you, my noble friend but I shall at once seek for employment. I shall not long remain idle; my capital is too small for that !"

" Well, of course, and I'll lend you a hand to find it. We'll go over and see the owners this afternoon; but if you get a ship, why can't you leave your sweet little lily and her buds with my Fanny? Fanny has no company except little Freddy and Bella, when I'm gone."

" I fear they would be too much trouble, and—"

" Trouble," interrupted Bowline; " talk of trouble to the marines, when pipe-clay is scarce and rations scant; but don't go for to tell me that pleasure is trouble !"

" But—"

" Oh, don't *but*, nor hem, nor haw about it, I know what you was agoin' to say. You was agoin' to palaver about expense and all that, but we can fix that without making a fuss. We'll let your wife, and the babies, and the she nigger, have all the room they want, and we'll let you pay your part of the mess-bill just as you would aboard ship, if we were sailing in company!"

"We'll, my good friend, to this arrangement I can no longer object. It shall be as you wish, and I acknowledge that it will much lessen my sorrow at parting with my wife, to know that she has dear good friends near, to protect and cheer her up in my absence."

"All's settled, wife!" shouted Bowline, gleefully, as his wife came in to set the table. "Mrs. Edmiston is to stay with you altogether, while him and me are off on our cruises."

"I'm glad of it, John; for indeed she seems like a dear, sweet creature! She shall be as a daughter to me."

At this moment in rushed little Freddy, with his hands and pockets full candy, followed by his sister, both of them looking so glad and happy, that one who loved them might almost wish to have them die then, in their bliss, before the pain of sorrow, and the clouds of anguish, and earth's dark misery, should fall upon them.

"Where's my babies, papa? I want to make 'em eat, now!" shouted the happy youngster, as he looked around, and then hearing

(3)

the cry of one of them in an inner room, off he bounded in search of them.

And now, for the present, we will leave this happy cottage, although our pen shall still cruise in the vicinity.

CHAPTER V.

A pair of men, cool, calculating, shrewd,
Who ever are in money-making mood,
Always ready for a trade or barter,
Quick alike to sell or make a charter,
Yet true and faithful in all their dealings,
With some mean, but many noble feelings,
Are those of whom we next shall scribble,
The Boston firm of " Brothers Dibble."

READER, permit me to introduce to you the owners of the ship Prescott, Mr. Samuel Dibble and his brother, Elihu. Behold them in a small counting-room in the third story of a large store, which stands near the end of.———— wharf. They occupy this small and lofty room, because they wish to save all the room they can, to stow their merchandise away in, for they are also heavy importers as well as owners of a large shipping interest. The room is small and dusty, and around the walls are pasted up all kinds of cards and advertisements. A very small cast-iron stove stands in one corner, in the centre of the room stands a desk, made on the matrimonial principle; that is, it is joined, having a shelf or ledge for writing on each side, and a case in the centre with pigeon-holes on both sides, all of which were filled with papers; some, dark, yellow, musty, and dusty—others, fresh and clean, with the ink scarcely dried on them. This desk was made to save room too. On its top was a pile of ledgers and dusty books. On either side, with their feet meeting underneath, and so seated that by inclining their heads a little around the corner, they could see each other, were seated the brothers Dibble, on two small three-legged stools. We have been thus particular in describing the counting-room of this firm, only because they were amongst the richest men of their city, and lived in magnificent dwelling-houses, and we wished our readers to know the contrast between a merchant's " place of business" and his residence.

We will now describe the brothers. Elihu, the eldest, was about fifty-three years of age, with a small but quick glancing gray eye, very nearly bald, and the little hair which was left upon the lower part of his head quite gray. His face was thin, his nose sharp, and his head seemed supported upon the upper edges of an enormous shirt-collar, which being stiffly starched, was set firmly under the lobe of each ear, the points coming to a point in advance of his face, three inches or more. His dress was a thread-bare suit of Yankee-made chocolate-coloured cloth; low shoes neatly tied with a piece of black cotton tape, and properly blacked with an application of tallow and amp-black.

The other brother looked about five or six years younger, had eyes of about the same size and colour, a face more full and ruddier, especially in the immediate vicinity of the nose, which was neither Roman nor Grecian in shape, although, in size and appearance it might be thought somewhat of the order " *Rum-un*," and was decidedly a " *turn-up*." In fact, although he was anything but *green*, he might be considered humanly *vegetable*, his hair being *carroty*, and all his teeth, except a few *roots* and *stumps*, having gone to *seed* or somewhere else. His dress was very similar to that on his brother's tall, lean figure, although a trifle more neat and spruce. He, too, was more portly than the other, but though they differed in form and feature, still in expression they were strangely alike. In both of them you could read the written proof of curiosity, calculation, speculation, and a few more of the peculiar *ations* of the great Yankee nation. Their eyes could at a glance dive into a man's business-box and read his thoughts and capacities: at a glance they could tell the worth of anything, from a box of real nutmegs to a cargo of green hyson, and how much profit could be realised therefrom. But enough of their looks.

When we permitted the reader to invisibly enter their counting-room, they were examining the papers of the Prescott, Captain Bowline's ship.

" The Prescott has made a fine trip—I see by her freight list and cabin register, a tarnation good un !" said the elder brother to Samuel Dibble.

" Wall, I reckon yes ! Purty consider'ble ! That Jack Bowline is a purty cute sort of a skipper, and—"

" Come in !" said Elihu, as a rap at the door announced some visiter.

The dusty old door creaked upon its hinges and Captain Jack Bowline and his friend, Mr. Edmiston, entered.

" How do du, Capting ? Wall, I do declare !" said Elihu, " I've hearn tell that if you speak of the Old Harry, that he's sure to be anigh you ! We was jist a talkin' about you and what a good voyage you'd made this time. I guess this trip will net us about four thousand, seven hundred, and thirty dollars and—"

" You're a little wrong, brother Elihu," interrupted Samuel; " we shall clear by the whole voyage, jist four thousand, seven hundred, twenty-seven dollars, thirty-nine and one-half cents."

" Wall, I want much out of the way, but every little is something !"

" I want to introduce my friend, here, Mr. Edmiston, to you, gentlemen !" said Bowline.

" Glad to see you, sir !" said both brothers cordially; and then Samuel, looking at the list in his hand, continued—" Edmiston, Edmiston—why you'd a passenger of that name aboard ?"

" Yes, sir, and this is he."

" Ay, ay !" said the merchant, " cabin passage—full price—paid cash—it's all right—all right—glad to see you, sir—stranger here? Glad to show you round, when I've got time—very busy just now, though!"

" Thank you, sir," replied Edmiston, " but I have a greater inclination for business than sight-seeing at this time."

" Right again, sir; all right—business before pleasure, is an old saying and like old wine, sir, all the better for its age! Like wine, sir? Got some fust rate, for two seventy-five a gallon!"

" Thank you, sir, I seldom use wine. I have called upon you, with my friend Captain Bowline, to see if you have any of your East India ships in, that are doing nothing. I want—"

" Oh, yes, we've got two A 1 ships at the wharf, sir—want to charter, sir?"

" No, sir, but I wish get the command of the first ship you send to sea!"

" Oh!" said Elihu, " is that all?"

" Oh!" echoed Samuel, " don't want to charter, eh?"

" No, sir, I am no merchant. I am only a sailor."

" And as good a one as ever trod a deck or squinted at the sun through a sextant!" said Bowline.

" Why, we might be a goin' to send a ship to sea purty soon, sir, and then we mightn't—and—"

" Oh, you needn't and, nor but, nor parleyvoo about it, Mr. Dibble!" said Bowline, warmly. " You have got two ships layin' alongside o' Long Wharf adoin' nothin', and no captain to 'em. I want you to give my friend, Captain Edmiston, lately Captain of the finest frigate in the Royal Navy, charge of the first ship you send to sea! If you don't, Jack Bowline quits your employ. Captain Edmiston is a man and a sailor, and I'm his security for all that!"

" Royal Navy—frigate—capting, eh?" asked both brothers, with evident confusion.

" Yes, captain of a frigate," said Bowline, in answer, most emphatically.

" Why," said Elihu, " you've taken us all of a sudden with your offer and all that, we'll consider and calculate a little—and Admiral —I mean Commodore—no—Capting Edmiston, if you and Capting Bowline will dine with us in Beacon-street, to-morrow, we'll have a talk and may-be we may conclude to make some sort of a kind of a bargain!"

" Yes, do come," added Samuel, " and you shall drink some of the best old wine that ever tickled the ceiling of your windpipe, or lit up warm feelin's in your buzzoms! We dine at three exactly, and we never wait a minnit for nobody!"

" ' We'll be there in time,' as the sinner said to the devil, when he invited him to go below with him!" answered Bowline; " but, gentlemen, you may just make up your minds to take Captain Edmiston into your employ or to let me out of it. If you don't give him a ship, why just go and hunt up another Captain for the Prescott. I've said my say, and I mean it!"

"Wall, come to dinner to-morrow and we'll see if we can't hit on a bargain!" said Elihu.

And to make the bargain we will leave them, reader, while we take another trip back to old England and see how Lord Hawkhurst is getting on with his broken thigh and Dr. Gangrene's "undivided," and personal and scientific attention.

CHAPTER VI.

On all the passion-tide of life
There floats no bark
With sin so dark,
So wild, so mad, with hell so rife,
As that which bears the pennon red
Of fell revenge at its mast-head ;
With ebon sail
It woos the gale,
Nor furl nor reef can stay its wrath,
No obstacle obstructs its path.

"WELL, sir, the forty days have elapsed; the period you set for my recovery, and here am I in this infernal bed yet !" said young Lord Hawkurst to Doctor Gangrenge, angrily, just forty days after the interview which the reader had with him in the second chapter.

"We can in a most scientific and satisfactory manner account for the delay in your convalescence, my lord."

"Well, sir, how can *we* do it ? *we* would like to have a satisfactory explanation !"

"It is owing, in a great measure, my lord, to the nervous excitement and agitation produced by your permitting yourself to get into a passion so often, and drinking more than three diminutive glasses of port wine per day, and also—"

"To the devil with your *ands* and your *alsos*, and you too, you old humbug ! I will not be cooped up here swallowing your quack nostrums any longer."

"Quack ! quack, did you say, my lord ?" angrily retorted the doctor. "Quack ! the owner, possessor, proprietor, and deserving recipient of *seven diplomas*, all written in Latin, on parchment, and tied with green ribbons—"

"To show that they who gave them to you were *green !*" again interrupted the impatient patient.

"Sir ! My lord, we mean, we cannot, will not submit to this indignity ! it is too much—too much !" and the horrified physician fell back upon the sofa as red as a lobster, and declared that he would faint, and that he would call for satisfaction.

"Oh, well, you can have that as soon as you please, but you've got to get me well enough to stand up for you; that's a consolation. What weapons will you choose, lancet, or mortar-pestle—eh ?"

"My lord, don't get into a passion, now; keep cool, as we do—keep cool—we are perfectly cool, and we won't fight you! No, my lord—we—we will only dress your leg for you."

"*Only! We* think you *only* will, if you only get an only chance. Make out your bill, sir, and then make yourself out of my sight! —Ah, Clare, I'm devilish glad to see you!" continued the young lord, as his friend entered the room. "I want you to kick this old humbug out of my sight."

"I'll sue you for slander; you called me quack, sir! humbug, sir! and talked of kicking, sir. I'd like to see you kick me, sir! I dare you to kick me, sir!"—now shouted the doctor, forgetting his "we" of dignity in his anger.

"Clare, just render me a personal obligation, by being my proxy in this case, and kick that infernal impudent scoundrel out of the room!"

"Certainly," replied the accommodating friend, and as promptly did he proceed to carry the desire into execution. But he had formed a rather hasty opinion of the doctor's pluck, for the latter, on feeling the unpleasant application of Mr. Clare's foot, suddenly turned around, and planted a blow in his face, which sent him reeling to the floor, while the red blood gushed in torrents from his nose and mouth. And not satisfied with simply knocking his insulter down, he at once leaped astride of his fallen foe, and, in a most scientific manner, proceeded to administer sundry and many blows and punches, his knowledge of anatomy enabling him to pick out the tender spots. Oh, it was a funny sight to see the little, short-legged doctor, his very red face uncommonly red with anger, with his fat little fists beating the devil's tattoo upon poor Clare's head. Clare lay face down, half suffocated, crying, "Murder! take him off! Hawkurst, why don't you help me?"

"How the devil can I, when he has got me down as well as you? I have no strength in my leg to move with; the servants are all out—but here goes one of his own doses of quack medicine; I think that'll start him off you!" and with this, the invalid lord let fly a large phial of medicine, which stood within his reach, at the doctor's head. The latter had raised his head to look at the young lord, as he heard him say "quack," and the phial struck him full in the face, distributing its liquid contents plentifully into the eyes, mouth, and nose of the belligerent physician. And then, as Byron, or some one else, says—"how changed the scene!" With a perfect howl of agony, with both of his hands up to his face, as if he was trying to rub himself out, the doctor leaped up from his conquered antagonist.

"Oh, blood and thunder! The sal ammoniac! Hell and hartshorn! Throw water in my face! Murder, murder! Where's the door? Water! fire! help!" shouted he.

Staggering to the door, the doctor rushed out, upsetting two or three servants, who, attracted by the shouting, were hastening to the scene. Meantime, Clare had regained his feet, and stood a bruised, black-eyed, bleeding specimen of decently thrashed humanity, while Hawkhurst lay in his bed laughing immoderately at the tragico-comico affair.

"Devilish funny, 'pon my soul!" said he—"a capital joke, isn't it, Clare? Made the old dog sick with his own medicine; devilish good, isn't it, eh?"

"It may be funny to you!" said the other, savagely; "but I'd like to know whether I've swallowed a half dozen of my front teeth, or spilled them on the floor. How do my peepers look?

"Just like two holes burned in a yellow and red chequered blanket, only a little more so."

"By Jupiter, he shall suffer for it!" said the enraged victim.

"Oh, don't bear malice, Clare," replied Hawkhurst; "blood-letting and tooth-drawing are all in the line of his profession, and you have received his scientific, undivided, and personal attention!"

"None of your jokes, Hawkhurst! I didn't come here to joke—I had some news for you which I was about giving to you when you got me kicked into this devilish scrape."

"You kicked yourself into it, my boy—but you spoke of news; what is it?—have you heard from them, from *her?* Do you know where they've gone to—what place—where they are now?" added the impetuous invalid, his whole manner changing as the cloud of revenge again shadowed his countenance.

"Don't ask too many questions at once, and I'll answer you!" responded Clare.

"Well, well, go on. Have you heard from them?"

"Yes; they sailed in a packet-ship for Boston, and a ship that got into port from there yesterday, reports their safe arrival."

"Clare!" said Hawkhurst, with a strange but meaning emphasis, "you must go to Boston for me!"

"To Boston? me? Why, Hawkhurst, what are you dreaming of?"

"I'm not dreaming, or sleeping either, Clare. You must go to Boston at once, and get track of them until I am able to travel. They must not, shall not escape me!"

"I can't go so far away from home, Hawkhurst; I never was on salt-water in my life!"

"Well, you've got to go now; you know how I have befriended you, when no one else would have lent you a hand to keep you out of the gutter, and if you desert me now—"

"I will not desert you, Hawkhurst, but I hate this duty; I wish to heaven you'd let them go free now that they're out of your way!"

"Out of my way? Are they out of the world? The earth cannot give bounds to my revenge! It may be long before I can accomplish my aim, but so sure as my life is spared, that beautiful scorner of my passion shall kneel and sue at my feet for favour; that husband, he who revels in joys which I have coveted, he who triumphs in my present suffering, shall die—die! I've sworn it, by the HAND that made me! Revenge is all that now is left me, and I will enjoy it."

"Well, have it your own way. How and when must I be off? You'll have to furnish the rhino."

"You must go in the first packet that sails, and I'll give you money enough to live in as good style as I would myself if I were there. By-the-way, I can fix it so that you'll have your own fun, for I'll send you over as a *lord*. You can gull the Yankees and enjoy the dignity of nobility at the same time. I can get you letters to their leading potentates, and perhaps you can win an heiress with a couple of hundred niggers and a cotton plantation—at any rate you can have your own fun, and at the same time have a better chance to gain my information for me."

"Capital, capital! Hawkhurst, I'm yours for ever, as Faustus said to the devil! Then I shall for once in my life live like a real lord, and be my-lorded—and all that?"

"Yes, I'll see to that at once. Bring me my check-book here, and do you take the money and fit yourself out well. Remember that you will go as a lord, and of course will be *lionized!*"

"Thank you, my lord, I'll support the honours. But it'll take plenty of rhino, for I intend to make a dash!"

"You shall have sufficient."

CHAPTER VII.

Now, by the power of our magic pen,
We'll waft the reader o'er the sea again;
And deeper dive into the mystery
Of this strange and wondrous history.

READER, you have seen the "Brothers Dibble" in their counting-room, that eight feet by ten business-coop which we briefly described in the fifth chapter, and now we wish you to pay them another visit.

Within a large and magnificent building which fronted upon that elm-shaded and (in the sweet summer time) lovely spot, known to the refined as the "Mall," and to the *common* as "Boston Common;" that sacred spot where the cherished "Tree of Liberty" spreads its iron-bound branches out over the sod which is rendered sacred by the many ties which history's noble record has bound around it. Within a princely mansion which stood before this memorable park, in a room magnificently furnished, a party was seated at dinner.

The "Brothers Dibble" were there of course, for this was their house, and Mrs. Elihu Dibble was there, (Samuel, the red-faced brother, was still a bachelor), a woman of not more than half her husband's age, but of fifty times more beauty; and Captain Bowline with his friend Edmiston completed the party.

They had finished the meat courses, and were engaged upon the dessert. Before Mr. Samuel Dibble stood a half-emptied decanter of old sherry, which was nearly as red and bright as his own countenance. But beside Elihu, the elder, was nothing but a simple glass of water, as pale and cold as seemed his own half-frozen blood.

"May I have the pleasure of taking another swig with you, Commo—I mean Capting Edmiston?" said Samuel, the younger brother, passing his decanter to his guest, for whom, as a late Captain in the Royal Navy, he seemed to entertain the highest respect.

"With pleasure, sir," replied the guest; "and I will propose to you a sentiment. 'America, the land of the free and the home of the brave; may her future prosperity be as bright as her past history has been glorious!'"

"Good, by gracious!" exclaimed the merchant, as he swallowed a bumper to the toast. "Mister—I mean Commo—no, I mean Capting Edmiston, if you are a Britisher born, you're a republican Yankee at heart, if you ain't, drat my buttons!"

"He will be a Yankee when he has the flag of our Union waving over his head, and stands on the quarter-deck of an American ship; and the sooner you give him a command the better it will be for you and him; that's my reckoning," said Bowline.

(4)

" Wall, we may as well go to talking about that, now," said Elihu, " for we sent for you to dinner a-purpose to see what we could do. The old sayin' is, 'business before pleasure;' but we go in for making a pleasure of business, and mixing our pleasure with business, as salt to the porridge—but, as I was a sayin,' we may as well have a talk about business now, as not."

" Yes," said the junior brother, " exactly so; but before you say anything more, Mister—I mean Capting Edmiston, take another swig with me. This ere grape juice is fust rate and no mistake, was bought in Maderia, in 1801, and cost two dollars and seventy-three cents a gallon, by the quantity, in wood, and—"

" I don't drink wine or know much about its quality," interrupted Elihu, at this moment; " but, brother Sam, you've made a mistake in the price of that 'ere wine. It cost just three dollars and eighty-three cents a gallon, by the quantity, in wood; and, making allowance for expense of bottling, wastage, and the interest of capital invested in it and lying idle, it is worth about seven dollars and three-and-six a gallon, now."

" Wall, maybe I did make a slip of eight or ten cents, and every little counts," replied the other.

" Yes, ten cents, exactly."

" Well, what about a ship for Captain Edmiston?" said Bowline rather impatiently.

" What'll he take a month in wages?" asked both brothers.

" All that you'll give, I suppose!" said Bowline, laughingly " but I'll let him answer for himself."

" I shall only ask the customary salary," said the person alluded to.

" Wall, the customary wages in this country is just as little as the employer can get a man to go for, and just as much as a man can get his employer to give him. It's a pull at both ends, and the one that can get the longest part of the string, keeps it," replied Elihu, who, having drunk no wine, was perfectly cool and ready for business.

" You will give me the command of one of your ships, then?" said Edmiston, his eyes brightening with hope.

" Yes, if we can agree as to wages. A man that's been a Captin of a frigate in the Royal Navy, sartingly knows how to handle ship; and if you're cute in business matters, I don't see why you shouldn't make a fust rate Capting. You see when folks know you've been a Capting in the Royal Navy, they'll be proud to go passengers with you; especially when they know you are a *lord's* son, and may be a lord yourself some day. Oh, you'll have a cabin full of passengers every trip!"

" Well, why don't you come to the *pint*, brother Elihu?" said Samuel, who had come nearer to his *quart* than a pint.

" Wall, 1 will, brother Sam; but keep cool, business is business you know, and business of this kind, like a lame horse, musn't be hurried. Capting Edmiston, we'll give you eighty dollars a month, and nothin' thrown in, except room to stow your private ventures at half the usual freightage, if you'll take charge of the ship Ruth, that now lays alongside Long Wharf, ready to fit out for a cruise to the East Indies."

"What say you to that?" said the junior brother, taking another glass of wine.

"I'll accept the offer!" said Edmiston, promptly.

"Wall, now that's jist what I like to see in a man, coming right slap down at once, yes or no; but it ain't the way of business, though. Take a glass of wine with you, Capting! Join us, Mr. Bowline?" cried the junior brother, evidently delighted with the low terms which Edmiston had engaged upon, and which neither of the brothers had expected he would accept.

"Yes, I'll join you in drinking success to Captain E. and the Ruth; but I think you are very mean in only giving him eighty dollars, to take charge of a seven hundred ton ship, when I get a cool hundred for sailing the Prescott!" answered Bowline, bluntly.

"If he's satisfied I'm sure you ought to be, Capting Bowline," said Elihu, rather tartly.

"Well, I suppose I ought to be; but I'd rather you'd just dock off twenty dollars from my salary and put it on his. He's as good a sailor as I am, every inch of him, and for a long cruise he ought to be as well or even better paid!"

"Brother 'Lihu, I guess we might afford to give Capting Edmiston a hundred; you know he has been in the *Royal* Navy, and—what did you get there?" said Samuel, his heart evidently warmed into generosity by the wine which he had drunk, which his brother's winks and frowns could not cool down.

"A little over forty pounds sterling a month, rations and all," answered Edmiston.

"What! More than *forty pounds sterling!* more than two hundred dollars a month?" exclaimed both the brothers in astonishment. "Why, what did you quit the Navy for?"

"Because I preferred independence to money."

"Wall, you *are* a trump—I'll take another glass of wine with you!" shouted Samuel, now beginning to show the evident effects of that which he had already swallowed.

"Let's have all settled about the wages first," said Elihu.

"Oh, darn it, he *shall* have a hundred!" shouted Samuel; "and if you won't give it, I will!"

"Out of your private pocket?" asked the cool and calculating Elihu.

"Yes, if you are so tarnal mean as to want me to do it!"

"Wall, brother Sam, as you're so positive, and Capting Edmiston has been in the Royal Navy, I guess I'll give in. He shall have the hundred, and I'll fit out the Ruth next week."

"Now you talk like a *white man*," responded the brother; "if you'd only join us in a glass of wine, you'd act like one !" responded the satisfied brother.

"I'm afear'd I'd look like a *red* man, as you do," said Elihu, "if I used the wine as free as you are adoing."

"Wall, it's my own; who has got a better right to it ?"

"Nobody, as I know of," responded the other; "but you and the two captings must excuse me and my wife, as we don't drink wine."

"Sarting !" said the junior; and the senior Dibble and his lady left the table.

As soon as they were gone, quite a load seemed to be taken off from the heart of the younger brother; and he shouted in great glee, "Now we'll have a time on it ! I never can act out, and feel right afore that sober-sided, water-drinking brother o' mine; but now we'll have a jolly time. Capting E., let's have a song !"

"I never sing, sir."

"Then Capting Bowline, sing us that jolly old stave of your'n, the one you call ' The Apology.' "

"I must, like my friend Edmiston, apologise for not singing, for it's getting late, and our wives and babies are waiting for us at home !" said Bowline.

"Wives and babies, eh? You ought to be like me, free from all such incumberances; but I didn't know that Capting Edmiston, late of the Royal Navy, had a wife—oh yes, I do remember, I saw a name of one Mrs. Edmiston on the passage list—passage paid—all right; but I didn't see no children mentioned !"

"They were born on the passage."

"Born on the passage? They! Why, how many of 'em was there? Have you got more than one wife, Capting?"

"No, sir; but the one that I have presented me with a sweet pair of twins on the passage."

"Rather expensive present, I reckon !" said the calculating merchant; his ruling passion being strong even in—liquor: and then he continued—"you're not agoin' to take your wife to sea with you, are you ?"

"No; I shall leave her ashore under the friendly care of my friend Bowline's wife, when I sail !"

"That's all right—all right, I never know'd a Capting do well when he carried his wimmen folks to sea with him. A woman aboard ship is as much out o' place as a rose in a tar-bucket. You're agoin' to leave her ashore, eh? Well, I'll keep a good look-out for her while you're gone, and introduce her into our society here. I expect they'll set a heap by her here, for of course she's a lord's daughter, bein' your wife !"

"We must leave you now," said Bowline, rising from the table, in which action he was joined by Edmiston.

"Wall, if you must, I s'pose you must—but you've got to take another glass with me afore you make tracks. Here's to them ere wives and babies o' your'n. May they—darn me if I know what to wish for 'em—may they get rich right off, and live as long as Methusalem!"

The sentiment was appropriately honoured, and then the parties separated.

Just two weeks after that dinner-party, Captain Edmiston tore himself away from his young and tender wife and beautiful babes, and sailed in the ship Ruth, from Boston harbour, bound to Batavia and an East India market. We need not dwell upon the mutual feelings of the separated parties; our cold pen would fail in the attempt. Mrs. E. was left with Mrs. Bowline, whose husband also sailed about the same time on his regular trip for London.

CHAPTER VIII.

Bow down, ye slaves and sycophants! bow down,
And show how tame and spiritless ye've grown
Since that forgotten day your ancient sires
First lighted up bright freedom's sacred fires;
Bow to the titles ye affect to hate,
Cringe in all the base servility of state
To the nobility of name and power!
And hath it come to this? oh, cursed hour,
When we forget the past and bend the knee
To those from whom our sires have made us free!
Blush, blush for shame, and hide each blushing face,
And ponder o'er your dark and deep disgrace!

"HAVE you hear'n tell?" said Samuel Dibble to his brother, as they sat together in their eight by ten foot counting-room about four months after the ship Ruth had sailed.

"No! What?" replied the sanctimonious Elihu, with an air of excited curiosity.

"Why, a lord, a real lord, has just come over in the last packet on a *tower* of pleasure through the country!"

"What! a real lord? What's his name?"

"They call him Lord Clarence, and they say he eats out of gold plates and has got more money than he can keep count of!"

"Where does he put up? We must go and see him and ask him to dinner! When he goes back we must offer him a free passage in the Prescott, and then won't she be full of passengers?"

"She won't be anything else," was the laconic answer of the elder.

"Wall, I wonder—" commenced Samuel; but his remark was interrupted by a knock at the door, and he simply added—"Come in."

"Ah, how-dee do, Mister Bilbo—how-dee—glad to see you! What's news—eh? all well to hum, eh?" cried both brothers, to the person who entered—a tall, fat individual, with a consequential look, and a face which, in its ruddy hue, threw Mr. Samuel Dibble's quite in the shade.

"Yes, all well—" replied the individual,—"but such news!— I've come for you!"

"For us? What's the matter—nobody dead?"

"Oh, no, no! but there's a lord come to town—a real lord, and we must pay his excellency all due attention. We must go in a committee and call on his lordship, and give his excellency a dinner and invite his majestic graciousness to a dance, and turn out the trainin' company to fire a *few-de-joy*, as the Frenchers call it, for him—and you must be on the committee, and we must do things up brown!"

"Why we were just a talkin' of that 'ere chap when you come in!" said Samuel.

"Oh, everybody is a talkin' of him—he's agoing to be the lion of the day—it ain't often that a real lord comes over here to see us, and we must make hay while the sun shines!"

"That's a fact," said Elihu; "when is the committee to meet, Mr. Bilbo?"

"Right straight off now directly, at the old Marlboro'—put on your hats and come along."

"Oh, we must slick up a little fust—put on clean dickies and Sabberday clothes—it wouldn't do to go to see a lord right out of the office in this 'ere fix!"

"Wall, you go and slick up and I'll meet you at the Marlboro' with the rest, in an hour from now, I reckon."

"Wall, we'll be there."

And then the parties at once separated, to prepare to pay their respects to Lord Clarence, of England.

We will, however, get ahead of them in their visit, reader, and at once pay our respects to this distinguished individual, who, (be it a secret between us) is neither more, less, or other than Mr. James Clare, the friend and tool of Lord Hawkhurst.

In the best parlour of the old Marlboro' inn, at the same moment when Messrs. Dibble and Bilbo were preparing to pay their ceremonial visit, James Clare, or Lord Clarence as we must now call him, reclined upon a settee which, with flower-painted back and green cushions, had stood there from the time whereunto extended the memory of the oldest inhabitant. He was much altered, and somewhat improved from his appearance when we last saw him as he arose after receiving a pummelling from the skilful hands of Dr. Gangrene. His fine-featured face had received the addition of a jet black beard and moustache of some four months growth; his hair had been suffered to grow, and now hung in rich curls down a neck which was so well-turned and white, that he prided himself on wearing an open collar, à la Byron: his dress was more rich and gaudy than tasty, as is usually the case with those who are enabled to imitate gentility, without possessing its innate principle.

Although it was prior to the dinner hour, and decidedly un-fashionable, the psuedo lord held a half-emptied tumbler of grog in his hand, while at intervals he raised a fragrant cheroot to his lips and lazily watched the blue wreaths of smoke as they floated up to the low white-washed ceiling.

He rung a bell which lay upon the window ledge by his side. It was answered by the appearance of a servant dressed in gaudy livery.

"Did you call, my Lord?" asked the man, in a broad English accent.

"Yes, John, I wish to know how many dem'd republican cards have been left this morning?"

"Over a hundred, my Lord!"

"You took good care to impress the uncivilized creatures with a proper estimate of the honor we do them in our visit to their dem'd wild country?"

"Yes, my Lord, and they seemed very impatient to see your Lordship."

"Ah, dem them, let them learn patience! When we honor them with a visit, they should be made duly sensible of our dignity!"

"Yes, my Lord. Is there anything more you wish at present?"

"No, John. You may leave. I'll ring when I want you."

The door had hardly closed upon the retreating form of the servant, when the pseudo lord burst out into a scornful laugh.

"This, indeed, is well!" said he. "My lordship is well pleased, demnition well pleased, and the pleasure is dem'd cheap. I only have to watch the motions of a pretty woman and her husband, and receive the homage of the unwashed democracy. By-the-way, thinking of that husband, I must keep a bright look out for him, or he may detect my disguise and give me trouble. He never saw me but once, and that was on the foggy morning when the duel took place; he will not be very apt to remember me. Oh, what's wanting, John?" continued he, as the servant again entered.

"There are thirteen gentlemen down below, who have called to see your lordship, and insist upon being presented."

"Oh, tell them to go to the devil; I can't be disturbed until I recover somewhat from the fatigues of my voyage!"

"But, my Lord, they wished me to say to you that they were a committee on the part of the city—"

"A committee?"

"Yes, my Lord, a committee of citizens."

"Well, I suppose I must condescend to receive a committee. Remove this liquor, and then admit them."

"Yes, my Lord."

The next moment the servant ushered into his lordship's presence, the deputation of whom Mr. Bilbo was the leader, and the "Brothers Dibble," members, in company with ten others of the "leading men" of the town. Mr. Bilbo appeared to have been selected as the spokesman, for as the party entered the door with a profusion of low bows, and grimaces of respect, and walked about half way across the room, he opened his battery.

"Glad to see your lordship's excellency, and give ye a hearty welcome to Bosting—committee of thirteen, your Lordship's graciousness, to represent the thirteen States, which feel honored by your majestic goodness's presence! Want you to accept a public dinner, your lordship, and see our new trainin' company, your lordship." And here the speaker paused, evidently out of breath from the rapidity of his vocal labour.

"Thank you, sir, on your own part, and also for this attention from your fellow citizens. We shall remain for a short period in your city, and will take pleasure in accepting your proferred hospitality."

"Thank your lordship's most gracious excellency—you do us proud."

"Be seated, gentlemen, be seated," interrupted the noble lord; and as they with a profusion of bows and thanks located themselves in as close proximity to him as possible, he added—"Permit me to order some wine and refreshments—John, attend to it directly."

"How very nice his lordship does act!" whispered Bilbo to his next neighbour, who passed the whisper on until it had been re-echoed by each of the party.

In a moment more, waiters entered bearing some wine.

"Now, gentlemen, permit me to drink your very good healths," said the noble lord.

"The same to your lordship's excellency!" said Mr. Bilbo, and the rest as in duty bound echoed his response.

"You do not all join me!" said Lord Clarence, as his eye glanced upon the elder Dibble and two other pale-faced members of the committee, who did not drink.

"No, your lordship's majesty must excuse Mr. Dibble and Deacon Rant and his brother John; they have conscientious scruples in regard to drinkin' ardent sperits and—"

"I'll always drink brother 'Lihu's share!" interrupted Mr. Samuel Dibble, suiting the action to the word, and raising his second glass to his lips. "My lord, I'm agoin' to give you a toast in answer to your'n, and I hope you'll agree to join?"

"Certainly, sir, proceed."

"Wall, here's to trade, may it keep us and Old England a shakin' in the hopper of peace, till all the bran of discord is shook clean out of the grist."

"I join in your sentiment, sir, although it is couched in a phraseology, which I may say is all Greek to me!"

"What did your lordship observe about Greek, may I be so bold as to ask; for I'm acquainted with the leadin' principles of the language, bein' engaged in the district to teach the same?" said the before-alluded-to temperate brother of Deacon Rant.

"O, do hush yer yap and not be abringin' the school up afore his lordship's graciousness !" said Mr. Bilbo, with that emphatic dignity, which a new office too often gives. His lordship seemed evidently pleased at this interruption, for the schoolmaster's Greek might not have been more intelligible to him, than Samuel Dibble's miller slang.

"Let us attend to the business part of our visit, Mr. Bilbo !" said Dibble the elder, "I'm in a hurry—I always am, and business—"

"Is business !" continued the other, "so here goes. When will your lordship find sufficient leisure to attend a dinner which we'll give you in the Old Funnel, and—"

"What du you ask his lordship about leisure for ? He's a man of leisure ! Time ain't no more to him than fleas is to an elephant !"

"I'd just thank you, Mister Johnny Rant, to hold yer yap !" angrily cried Mr. Bilbo, and then continued; "I know that your lordship is a man of leisure, but we'd like to suit your convenience as to time and everythin' else !"

"Thank you, sir, I will make my time bend to your wishes. I shall remain some time in your city, and wish to become acquainted with your manners and customs. From that which I have already observed I perceive that you are a people of peculiarities !"

(5)

"Yes, your lordship, we have a good many *arities* and *r*
amongst us !"

"How soon does your lordship think of goin' hum to E
again ?" asked the elder Dibble, evidently bent on "busines

"Well, sir, I cannot tell at present—perhaps in a month (
perhaps not for a year; but may I inquire why you ask ?"

"Oh, yes, your lordship; I only wanted to know, bec
wanted to tell your lordship that you might go over in the Pr
and it shouldn't cost you a red cent !"

"The Prescott ?" asked the other quickly. "The Presc(
she not a regular packet between this port and London ?"

"Yes, your lordship, and me and my brother there—S;
look up, his lordship is a talkin' to us—are the owners of h

"Ah, I'm glad to meet you !" said Clarence, as hi;
brightened with pleasure. "Did a passenger named Edi
come over in her a few months since ?"

"Oh, yes, he, and his wife; and they—I mean she, had—

"Where are they now ?" hurriedly interrupted Clarence, s(
concealing his anxiety.

"Why, the Capting is at sea on an East India trip, in one
ships, and his wife and babies are over in Charlestown, al
mile and half, or three quarters, from here. Your lords
acquainted with 'em, I reckon."

"Yes—no—that is to say, that I know him slightly, but :
friend of my friends !"

"Wall, I'm glad to hear o' that, for his lady will be right ;
see one of her countrymen here. She's a perfect lady—a
daughter, and I s'pect she's right lonesome here, poor creete

"Does she go much into company ?"

"No, your lordship, but I'll take you over to see her a'mc
time you'll go !"

"Thank you, I shall take pleasure in making her acquai
for her husband's sake."

"Wall, I'll call, in my shay, for you a'most any time !"

Their conversation was here interrupted by Mr. Bilbo, wl
been conversing apart with the rest of the committee, abo
time and manner of entertaining his lordship, who said—

"We'll send your lordship word as soon as we get things fi
entertain your lordship."

"Very well, sir, I shall be pleased with your pleasure !
morning, gentlemen."

"Good morning to your lordship's gracious excellency,
Mr. B. and the committee; and as they literally backed out
presence, bowing as they went, they whispered each to the o
"What a very nice lord he is ! How condescendin' and p
He's e'en-a-most like other folks, 'ceptin' he is a lord !"

No sooner had they disappeared, than Clarence threw l
back upon the settee with a laugh of exultation—

"Surely, Fortune, the blind old witch, is on my side!" soliloquized he. "Here I am at once upon the track without any trouble. The wife is here, the husband is away, and I can fix everything to suit Hawkhurst's aims exactly. I must write immediately and get further orders—meantime keeping an espial over her, and receiving the attendance of these vulgar Yankees!"

CHAPTER IX.

Revenge may be by fate delayed,
But yet its flame will burn as strong ;
For know ye not that hate when stayed,
Hath time to plot a double wrong ?
Ay, like the fuel on the hearth,
It makes in coals a fiercer fire
Than when, in sickly flames, its birth
Threw smoke and light a little higher.

ONE month later in our history.

Lord Hawkhurst, although still confined to his room from the effects of his wound, was able by the aid of his cane to limp about the carpet and look out upon the garden, which in all the rich beauty of summer's ripe blossomings lay beneath his window.

His impetuous spirit but ill brooked his bodily confinement, and to thus gaze out upon the bright, glad scene before him, without the power of tasting its fresh enjoyments, only added fuel to the fire of his impatience.

"A curse on him who thus crippled me!" said he, in a deep tone of bitterness. "A curse on my unsteady hand that did not meet his aim with aim as true! Why does not Clare write to me? He too is a laggard, or perhaps in his new-born station has forgotten to do his master's bidding."

A step was heard entering the room, and the speaker paused and turned towards the door.

"The morning's mail, my Lord," said the servant; and as he laid a parcel of letters and papers on the centre table he bowed and retired.

"The mail? Ah, well, let me see what is in it. Ah, a document from the Commissioners, with the Admiralty seal upon it!"

Hurriedly the young lord broke the seal, but as he perused the contents of the letter, his brow grew dark with angry vexation.

"What is this?" he cried; "orders to take command of the Hermione, and proceed to the East Indies! What! and delay my plans of revenge? No! never! never! I will sooner resign my commission, so that's settled; and now I'll see what more news the devil has sent me. Ah, here is a letter with the American ship-mark upon it—Clare is faithful. I did not think he would dare to deceive me!"

Then, as he hastily opened the letter and glanced over its con-

tents, more bright and glad glistened his eyes, a smile of exultation replaced the frown which had hung like a cloud upon his
countenance.

"Oh, 'tis well indeed!" said he. "The husband and wife are
apart, and both shall feel my revenge. She is safe under the
watchful eyes of Clare, who must soon change his disguise, but he
—he shall be my first victim, and through him I'll strike the first
blow to her heart. He sails to the East Indies. 'Tis well; the
order which but a moment since I cursed, is now the dearest boon
which I can crave from the government. I'll go and first meet
him; then for her and my last triumph. His ship is the Ruth.
She will sail to Batavia, and thence to Canton. And he, late a
Captain in the Royal Navy, is now the paltry skipper of a merchantman. Oh, heaven, my revenge is short and sweet, but yet it
is not half complete. I must write to Clare immediately. He
must keep a watch over her, and at the proper time abduct and
bring her here, where on my return I can once more kneel at the
proud lady's feet and sue for a smile to cheer my breaking heart!
Oh, God! to think that I, I have bent my pride to this, and yet
been spurned and scorned! But I bide my time and it is coming.
Let me see—by Clare's letter I see that Edmiston sailed some
time since. He will be on his return from his first voyage before
I can reach the station, but on his second voyage—then we will
meet and the first blow shall be struck. It may be near two years,
but were it fifty my hate would not sleep or my passion slumber.
Yes, I will obey the orders of the Admiralty, for they suit my
purposes!" For a little time the young lord passed up and down
the room, almost forgetting his lameness, in the hellish joy which
filled his heart. Again he paused and re-read Clare's letter.

" 'She is living in Charlestown, the place where we got so infer-
nally whipped by a party of raw militia men when the colonies
revolutionised. She is living with the wife of the captain of a
packet ship, and there are none but female servants in the house.'
So far, so good— ah, what's this? 'Herself, her negro nurse, and
two twin chil—' What! children? Roxanna Edmiston a mother?
But it is well—there are still more victims for my revenge! Again
his letter; 'the house is near the water's-edge, the town keeps but a
scanty night watch, she could be easily removed by force, if it is
necessary.' So much for that. Oh, Clare, you are a jewel of a
villain; but the time has not yet quite arrived. I must give him
some new instructions. He must change his disguise and be less
public. He has lorded it long enough; and change will be necessary for safety. But she shall rest for a while; he is my first
victim. By striking at the trunk or stem of a flower and cutting
off its sap, you quickly deaden the flower which hangs above. Cold
and bitter has been my wrong; dark and direful shall be its
recompense!"

CHAPTER X.

Deeper and deeper still the mystery ;
Stranger and stranger still my history ;
But follow on each dark and winding turn,
And with each hasty step new things you'll learn.

" I do wonder !" said Elihu Dibble to Samuel, his brother, as they sat at their twin desk, pen in hand, one clear morning early in the autumn of 1822.

" So do I! what is it ?" replied the other, raising his eyes and pen from the leaf of a ledger in which he had been making entries.

" Why, what could have taken off Lord Clarence in such a hurry, without his even calling to say good-by to us, or tell us when he was a comin' back agin ! I do think it was tarnal shabby treatment after we've been to the trouble and expense of entertainin' him so grand !"

" Wall, it does seem a leetle hard, brother 'Lihu, but I s'pose he was in a hurry to git off on his *tower* and wanted to go ' *incognighto*,' as the schoolmaster says, meanin' I s'pose that his name and title is to be kept as dark as the cog wheels of night, or somethin' o' that ere sort !"

" Wall, but he might have told us; we would a kept his secret as close shut as we would our own money-safe. I wonder if he ever said good-by to Mrs. Edmiston ? He was very attentive to her !"

" Yes, a heap more so than she was to him. She didn't treat him a bit better than she did me, nor even quite so perlitely, even though he was a lord."

" Wall, she's a lord's daughter, you know, and used to seein' real lords every day ; and, besides, you know she's bound to treat us well bein' as we are the owners."

" That's a fact—but business is business; let's see—the Ruth sailed just five months and thirteen days ago ; if she has good luck she ought to be home in about as much more time. I think Capting Edmiston can make as quick a trip in her as anybody else. He talked like a real sailor, but he did want a few too many instruments. Just to think of his taking a chronometer and a six hundred dollar one at that. Why, old Capting Bunker went that same voyage over twenty times, and never carried anything but his old rusty quadrant !"

" Yes, but he hadn't been in the Royal Navy and learned to use all the fancy gimcracks that'll tell jist where the ship is and ought to be and all that !"

" No, but he made quick trips and big profits for all that."

" That's a fact—but I do wonder what keeps the Prescott behind her time. She'd ought to have been here two days ago, with the winds that have been blowin' from the east'ard for the last ten days. I do won—"

"Come in !" said the other brother, as a hasty knock at the door announced a visitor.

"Wall, I never ! How true that ere old sayin' is : talk of the old Harry and he's stark sure to pop up afore your face ! Why, Capting Bowline, we were just a talkin' about you. How do you do ?"

"Hearty as a middy on duff day !" replied the Captain, for it was the veritable Bowline himself. "How are ye all ? Here's the old craft's papers, overhaul them and see that all's right. I must make sail for Charlestown to see the wife and babies."

"Wall, but do tell us—"

"O, I'll tell you in the morning, all that you want to know, but you might as well ask my mainmast to sing you a love song as to try to get anything more out o' me ,till I've seen how all goes on at home !" and away dashed the warm-hearted sailor to the spot where the sheet anchor of his heart lay, leaving the owners to look over the papers and calculate the amount of their profits.

CHAPTER XI.

There is a joy when lovers meet
Which words would all too faintly tell ;
There is a joy when old friends greet,
Which makes each heart responsive swell.
But higher, fiercer, wilder yet
Than tongue can speak or pen can write,
That hellish joy when foes have met
To end their hate in deadly fight ;
When face to face and hand to hand,
Their clashing steel rings loud and high,
And firm as rocks they sternly stand
Where one or both must surely die.

BEAUTIFUL, oh ! how beautiful was the night when the ship Ruth, Captain Edmiston, entered the straits of Sunda, on her third voyage to Batavia. The sea was running in that long, regular swell, which is only produced by the trade winds of long continuance, and the noble ship, with all her canvass set and drawing full, was climbing over the huge blue waves, now with her bowsprit pointing toward the skies, mounting up the mountain side of the blue roller, which, in the bright light of the full moon, glittered like a moving sheet of silver; then as swiftly rushing down the opposite steep; oh, it was beautiful !

The ship was now within three or four days' sail of her port, whither she was bound for a load of coffee, and, as they had already had a glimpse of the land off Java Head, the crew were in great glee. As the ship swept on in her noble grace, from her decks arose the jubilant songs of the mariners, who, in a breeze so fair and steady, had but little labour to attend to.

With a calm and satisfied look, Captain Edmiston paced up and down his deck, in company with his first officer, Frank Darlington; a noble fellow who was now on his third voyage in the same ship.

Although nearly three years have elapsed since Captain Edmiston took charge of the Ruth, time and exposure have made but a slight change in his appearance. He may indeed be a trifle darker, for the sun of the tropics has an embrowning habit, but his form is as full, his eye as bright, and his step as buoyant as when we saw him, a happy father, treading the deck of the packet-ship Prescott.

"What a happy set sailors are, take 'em in a lump!" exclaimed Darlington, the thought probably awakened by the noisy glee of the watch on deck, who were singing some lively chorusses.

"Yes, and yet it seems strange that they who are for ever absent from the ties and joys which usually endear men to life, who are deprived of so many of life's comforts, who are always exposed to peril and hardship, who are so often forced to stare grim death in the face, should meet all things with a laugh and suit themselves to all emergencies as they do!"

"Yes, Captain, it is strange, so strange that those who know them not, always deem sailors *thoughtless* beings, men who are fearless of danger because they think not of death, and yet how unjust it is to call them *thoughtless!*"

"It is, indeed. Few have more time to think, or better subjects to awaken thought than the sailor. How wide a range have we this night for thought. I, for instance, can let my mind wander back to my home, where I have left my angel wife and her dear little prattlers, who have scarce yet learned to lisp the name of father. I can in fancy see them all three kneeling in prayer to the Holy God of the Universe, the hands of my sweet babes crossed on their gently heaving bosoms, while their mother's pure soft lips send up her nightly prayers for my protection; and you, Frank, can in fancy wander back to your noble lady love, and think that she is gazing up at that round moon which shines so brightly down upon the ocean, the same water-link which, though distant and lengthy, ripples upon the strand of her native village, and—"

"Sail-ho!" sung out the look-out, from the topmast cross-trees.

"Where away?" shouted the Captain, whose remarks had been thus suddenly interrupted.

"About two points on our starboard bow, sir,—a full-rigged ship close hauled, standing athwart our course!"

"I see her, sir," said the mate, "here she is just betwixt the foremast and the starboard shrouds!"

"Oh, yes, I see her now!" responded the Captain, "why, she's very close aboard; you've kept a poor look-out aloft there, or you'd have seen her before!"

"She's been running down in the wake of the moonlight, sir, and it blinded me."

"Very well, keep your eyes about you a little closer in future. These seas have too many junks and proas cruising about in 'em to allow us to keep a sleepy look-out!"

"She'll come within hail of us, sir," again remarked the mate.

"Ay, I believe she will. She is a frigate too, I see, by her double row of teeth. Hand me your trumpet, I'll stand by to answer her hail."

The strange sail, with her yards braced sharp up, close hauled on a wind, her larboard tacks aboard, came dashing down towards them with the white foam wreathing like drifting snow around her dark prow. As she neared them, her bow suddenly swept up to port, her sails shivered in the wind, and then from her deck came the hoarse hail—"Ship ahoy! Who are you—where from, and where bound?"

"Ship Ruth, Captain Edmiston, from Boston, bound for a market!" was the reply.

The next moment another voice from the frigate, clear and loud, without a trumpet like him who first hailed, shouted—"Heave to, sir, we wish to communicate!"

"By Jupiter, I know that voice!" said Edmiston to his mate, as he at once gave the necessary orders to reduce sail and bring his ship to the wind.

"A friend, I hope, sir?" asked the mate.

"We'll see directly!" was the brief answer of the Captain, but while he spoke his face settled down in a look of firm but angry resolution.

In a few moments both vessels lay nearly motionless upon the sea, although nearly half a mile apart, having been separated before the slow working merchantman could be hove-to. After a brief delay the regular sound of oars was heard as the man-o'-war's boat approached the latter. An officer wrapped in a sea-cloak was standing in her stern sheets, and in a moment after she had reached the ship's side he stood upon the quarter deck. As he opened his cloak and exhibited the uniform of a British officer, Edmiston seemed disappointed in seeing one to him a stranger.

"Have I the pleasure of addressing Captain Edmiston?" said the officer, politely saluting Captain E.

"If it be a pleasure, you have, sir!" responded the latter.

"Then, sir, I have the honour to present to you this note from my commander."

Edmiston took the note, and various were the changes of his countenance as he read it. "Again?" he muttered to himself. "Again—why will he thrust himself in my way!"

"I await your answer, sir," said the officer.

"Are you aware of the contents of this note, sir?" asked Captain E., sternly.

"No, sir," replied the officer — "Captain Lord Hawkhurst simply told me that it was an *invitation* of some kind or other!"

"Ah, very well, sir, a verbal answer will as well serve his Lord-ship as a written one, and such friends as we are ought not to stand upon ceremony. Convey my warmest regard to your Commander, and say to him that I am bound in to Batavia Roads, and should his ship find an anchorage in the same port, I shall be exceedingly gratified to accept his very kind invitation!"

"I will, sir; a fair evening to you."

"Good night, sir," and then in a moment more the boat was pulling rapidly back to the frigate, and the merchantman filled away on her course.

During the interview with the officer, Captain Edmiston's cold and studied politeness and stern demeanour had been noticed by Darlington, who now approached him, as with a thoughtful air he paced up and down the deck.

(6)

"Captain," said he, "I dislike to be an intruder, but from your manner I feel confident that something disagreeable has come athwart your course. You know that you can always depend not only upon my sympathy, but also on my assistance in all circumstances!"

"Thank you, thank you, Frank! I shall need your assistance, and in a most unpleasant duty. That *polite invitation* was only a challenge to mortal combat from the bitterest foe I have ever had, one whom I have already had occasion to punish, but who seems determined that one of us must perish!"

"Who, and what is he?"

"Lord Hawkhurst, the commander of yonder frigate!"

"Has he just cause of quarrel?"

"Ile fancies so, I presume. We have met before; I was then the challenger and only crippled, when I might have killed him. You see how my mercy is rewarded."

"Yes, and it is so all over the world; kindness is but too often returned with ingratitude."

"You wi l have to be my second in this case, Frank."

"Certainly, if you must meet him; but I am opposed to the principle of duelling, and must hope that in this case it can be avoided."

"I know that it cannot, for he is as revengeful as the untamed savage of the wilderness. I wish that it could be avoided, for lonely and helpless would be my poor wife and babies if I should fall, but I musn't think of them."

"You should think of them before all other things on earth!" was the warm response of the noble Darlington, as the dew of sympathy glistened in his eyes.

"I do; I have!" responded Edmiston; "but though they are dear to me, my honour is even more dear to me. My wife had rather be a brave man's widow, than a coward's wife; and in this case, after having once challenged and fought him, it would be cowardly to avoid him when he seeks reparation."

CHAPTER XII.

Oh, villain, villain! though your deep disguise
The searching eye of careless man defies,
Though all doth seem to favour your design,
Beware! beware! there is a POWER divine,
Which ever shields the innocent and good;
Which tempers to their strength life's tempests rude,
And stretches forth its all-protecting hand
O'er them by night and day, on sea and land.

THERE is a beautiful walk on the borders of the little town of Charlestown, which is much frequented in the summer time. We allude to the borders of the river Mystic, which, leaving the bay, extends up from the Navy Yard, and winds along amongst the green knolls, we know not how far into the country.

As her little babes grew old enough to begin to toddle over the soft grass, and to tumble about among the flowers, this was a favourite summer evening stroll for Mrs. Edmiston. Attended by the faithful Judith, she frequently extended her strolls entirely beyond the borders of the town, and sometimes when the moonlight lay soft and sweet upon the waters, she forgot the usual tea-time hour and let night come on before she returned to the happy cottage of Mrs. Bowline.

In the summer of 1825, the first summer when Edward and Lettie, her sweet twins, began to lisp the name of their parents, this was her almost constant evening resort. She felt lonely, for her husband was absent on his third East India voyage, and though Mrs. Bowline was one of the kindest beings with whom God ever blessed the earth, yet she could not fill the void which Edmiston left in his absence. But her children had now become of that age which we may consider the most interesting to a parent; the moment, when as the bud of spring begins to gently part its outer leaf and show the colours within, they begin to exhibit the first signs of their nature and disposition; the moment when they require that tender care and careful guidance which no one but a mother can give.

How aptly may young life be compared to a flower. Take, for instance, one that groweth up amidst weeds and brambles, uncared for, untended, and unwatched; shaded perchance by the thorn and nettle, the sunlight hidden from its face until its very heart is chilled with the dark shadows which rest upon and around it, and it may blossom; but rough in its texture, coarse in its colours, without fragrance or beauty, ungainly in all things will be that flower. Take then another, which is planted in a well-cultivated garden, trained and watered by the hand of a prudent and careful gardener, shaded and protected from the rough storms, guarded from the vicious weeds which would start up around it, exposed properly and judiciously to the sunlight; and when it blossoms, how pure, noble, fragrant, and beautiful, it springs forth into the flower-world.   And yet one more simile quite as truthful as the two last.   Take a flower reared in a hot-house, reared with every care, but cultivated with artificial, and to it, foreign means.   It grows up and blossoms in rich but sickly beauty; and if it is exposed one moment to the common air of the world, it fades and dies.   But leaving the flowery, let us return to the reality of our story.

It was also in the summer of 1825, that the Prescott lay at the wharf ready for another voyage to London.   The cargo was all aboard, the crew shipped, light yards crossed, chafing mats aloft, and the ship only waited to fill up her passenger list and for a fair wind down the bay.   Captain Bowline and Ned Brace, his favorite old helmsman, who had now been promoted to the chief mateship of the vessel, were standing on the wharf alongside of the vessel, scanning her spars, sails, and rigging, to see if all was in sea-going order.

"The barkie looks fit for travel, don't she, Captain?" asked Brace, with a satisfied air, for he knew that but one answer would be given.

"Yes, she's all right, as right as a whale in deep water;—I guess she'll be making soap-suds outside by this time to-morrow.   If the breeze hauls off the land, I'm bound out either to-night, or early in the morning."

"Well, I don't see what on earth should keep us here except foul weather or bad luck, as the young wife said of her rich old husband; but I wish we had a few more passengers, if it was only for their company's sake."

"Is the Captain aboard?" asked a stranger, at this instant, of a sailor who was lashing a chafing mat on the after mizzen shroud, where the main brace passed it.

"He ain't aboard, but he isn't a great way off, sir!" said the Captain himself to the inquirer, who was a genteely dressed but strange-looking man, with red hair and whiskers, but exceedingly singular, in at the same time having black eyes.

"Are you he?" again asked the stranger.

"Well, I ain't nobody else, sir!   Do you want a passage?   We are agoin' to sail right away."

"How soon?"

"Just as soon as the clerk of the weather 'll send us a breeze—that's all we're waiting for now!"

"Then you'll sail to night!" said the stranger, as he glanced toward the west, and pointed at some clouds which were rising in that direction.

"Shouldn't wonder if we did!" was Bowline's reply, as he gazed for a moment upon the rising heralds of the breeze, and then, turning to his mate, he added—"Send up for Mr. Gurney, the pilot. Mr. Brace, the wind is coming fair and I must run home for a few minutes to say good-by, and then we'll slip our fasts and be out o' this."

"You can hold on until eight o'clock, for two passengers, can't you?" asked the stranger.

"Well, I might on a pinch," was the reply. "Why can't you get aboard sooner, though? I'd like to get out clear of the wharf afore dark!"

"Why, I have a sick sister to take over with me, whose case is so peculiar that it requires very careful management. In the first place, she is crazy, and the doctor has ordered that she sees no person but myself, and that she be not exposed for a moment to the light. She is, of course, a rather inconvenient passenger, requiring a darkened room by herself, and to have her meals prepared for her; but I am willing to pay a double passage, and I am her sole attendant."

"Poor creature!" said the tender-hearted Bowline. "Yes, we'll wait for her, and she shall have my own room, it is the largest aboard. Crazy, you said—poor creature—you sha'n't pay any double passage for her."

"Well, well, we'll not quarrel about the passage," replied the stranger, "but I must be extremely cautious to obey the orders of her doctor. She has to be closely veiled when she is moved, and it is necessary to carry her."

"Poor creature! it'll be hard getting her aboard, after we haul off, and I'd rather get off the wharf afore night."

"Oh, you can do that; I'll bring her alongside in a friend's boat; we have to bring her by water as it is: she is now staying at the house of one of my friends, on the Mystic river!" responded the stranger.

"Oh, well, if that's the case, then I'll haul off, and get ready to make sail. You'll be aboard by eight, sir?"

"Yes, or perhaps sooner."

"Very well, sir, I shall be all ready for you."

As the Captain made this remark, the stranger bowed and hurried away.

"I don't like that ere customer's looks, I don't, Captain Bowline!" said Ned Brace, as soon as the stranger walked away.

"Why not, Ned? I did'nt see nothin' strange except he had black eyes and red hair. He seemed to be pretty free with his money, offering to pay double passage for his poor sister, and I think that it's a pint in his favour to take so much care of the poor, helpless thing!"

"Well, he may be all right, Captain, but while he was spinning his yarn he didn't look you right in the eyes—his peepers kept cruising about, as if they were afeard o' contradicting his tongue. I wouldn't trust my father if he wouldn't look me in the eyes when he spoke to me."

" Well, we'll see what he's made of before the voyage is over.   I
must go home for a little while to say good-by.   You haul the ship
off into the stream, and have a boat sent for me at sunset.   Get
everything clear for sea—I shall get underway as soon as them last
passengers are alongside, for the breeze is freshening up a'ready."

" Ay, ay, sir !" responded the mate, and Captain Bowline hurried
homeward to take leave of his family.

When the stranger, who had spoken for a passage in the Prescott
that evening, left the wharf, he hurried along through several bye-
alleys and cross-streets until he got into Ann-street, along which
he passed a short distance and then entered a low frame house,
which denoted its character by the dingy red curtains which hung
inside of the windows.   Passing through the outer room, which
was filled with a drunken, noisy crowd of persons, black and white
of both sexes, and of the lowest order, he entered an inner apartment where were five persons dressed in the garb of sailors, engaged
at a game of " seven up," with brimming glasses of grog upon the
table around which they were seated.   As he entered the room,
they all rose respectfully.

" Champ," said he, to one of the most villanous, hangman-look-
ing of the lot.   " Champ, is all ready ; the boat and the mufflers ?"

" Yes, sir, all right as a trivet, and the hands here waiting your
orders !" answered the man.

" It is well, I shall need them to-night !"

" We are on hand, sir, for anything except church robbin', and
some of us wouldn't stick much at that !"

" Well, meet me with the boat at—no, I'll proceed by land to the
spot.   You know where the mouth of the Mystic empties into the
bay ?"

" Just as well as I know where my morning glass of grog empties
itself—you mean where the Eastern slope of Bunker's Hill runs
down to the water's edge."

" Yes, that is the spot.   You know that there are a few trees
near the point, and beneath them a green sodded walk."

" Yes, sir, it is a favourite walk for ladies, babies, and cattle, of a
summer evenin'."

" Well, be in that vicinity with the boat as soon as it grows dark ;
you know my whistle, when you hear it dash up with the boat—she
will be with me, and must be borne off in silence and safety to a
ship in the harbour."

" It's live stock that we're to smuggle to night, is it ?"

" Yes, and as it is your last job for me I shall pay you double."

" Long life to your honour," shouted the party in great glee at
the prospect of double pay.

" There, there, be quiet !" said the stranger ; and, as he turned
away, he added in a low tone to Champ, " It is your interest to be
faithful and discreet."

" I know it, sir, and you'll find me on hand."

It was twilight, soft, hazy twilight, and, though the black clouds flew by thick and fast overhead from the westward, still the water rippled gently along the grassy banks of the Mystic. The night shadows were gathering upon the waters, yet so still and quiet was the evening, so freshly and sweet came the soft land-breeze, bringing with it the scent of new-mown hay and flowers, that Mrs. Edmiston still lingered on her usual evening walk, along the green border of the river. She was accompanied by Judith and the two twins, Edward and Lettie, who were now able to totter over the short grass, and pluck up the wild flowers which met their glad young eyes.

Mrs. Edmiston had seated herself under the spreading branches of a large elm, which, with eight or ten others, stood near the water's edge, and was silently and sadly gazing upon the dancing wavelets of the bay, thinking perchance of him who was, she knew not where, but that he was distant, far distant from her side. Oh! it was well she knew not where he then was, else would she not have been thus calm and quiet.

"What a pretty boat! Eddy," said she, pointing out to the little one a boat rowed by five or six men, passing the point and, apparently, coming toward the landing near them.

"Pretty, Pretty!" lisped the blue-eyed boy, in imitative answer.

At this moment the lady heard a low long whistle near her, and then she saw the boat's prow turned directly in towards the land. While she gazed upon this manœuvre with a sudden presentiment of danger, a shadow fell upon the sod beyond her—the next instant she was seized in the arms of a rude strong man, and raised from the ground.

"Oh, God! Judith—the children! Fly! Oh, my hus—" screamed she; but her screams were stifled by the shawl which she wore being roughly pressed into her mouth. At the same instant the boat reached the land, and the man who had seized her rushed into it, bearing her along, and also the little Edward, who, with the tenacious grasp of frightened childhood, had clung to his mother's dress. Judith at first had started to run with the little Lettie; but, as she saw the boat shove off with her mistress, she rushed down into the water, shrieking and begging to be carried off with her lady, who had already fainted, and whom the stranger (for the reader will of course recognise him who had committed this outrage) was now engaged in binding and muffling, so as to disguise her to represent his sick sister.

"Curse this brat!—why was he brought into the boat?" said he angrily, as he saw little Edward clinging to his mother's dress, not crying, but with his blue eyes expressing angry astonishment; and then, after a moment's reflection, he added to the man who pulled the oar next to him, "Heave the brat overboard! He will spoil all!"

"No! no! don't kill the harmless baby! Give him to us, we'll take care of him," cried the crew with more feeling than one would have supposed them to possess.

" Well, take him and muffle him well, for with the first sound I hear from him, he goes overboard."

Still that young child wept not, nor screamed. They tried to tear him from his mother, and then his blue eyes flashed with anger, and he raised his little dimple hand and struck at them; but their strong hands tore his loose hold, and then he spoke:

" Oh, ma! ma!" in a voice so plaintive and touching that those rough smugglers' eyes filled with tears. But they bound him, wrapped him up in a rough pea jacket, and muffled his mouth; then they cast him under the thwart like a package of goods, and rowed swiftly down the bay. The hapless mother had partially recovered from her fainting fit, before they tore her child away; and as she heard his feeble voice, her clenched hands, and a quiver which ran over her beautiful form, betokened an agony, which words could not have expressed, even had she been able to speak. Oh, holy Heaven! what tongue could tell, what pen could write, what mind appreciate the fearful misery of that mother then? Torn from her babes, borne, she knew not where, reserved for, she feared a fate far, far worse than death!

The boat swept swiftly down the bay, and soon was alongside the Prescott. The helpless and muffled-up form of the female was passed on board, and carried down to a state room by the boat's crew. Then the stranger handed Champ, their leader, a bag of gold.

" This," said he, " is even more than you bargained for; but my success will permit me to be liberal. Silence and discretion."

" Ay, ay, sir!" was the low response of the smuggler; and, in a moment more, he and his crew had returned to their boat, and were rowing up the bay.

The next moment the cheerful " Heo heave, and up she comes!" of the ship's crew was heard, as they hove apeak their anchor, and in a few minutes the ship Prescott was standing down Boston harbour, with a fair wind, under a press of canvass.

CHAPTER XIII.

One night ! O, who may tell
The fearful deeds of hell ·
With which its records swell,
The anguish and the wo ;
O, whom save GOD may know ?

WHAT an eventful night to four of the characters in this drama was that in which closed our last chapter.

Mrs. Edmiston in the power of a ruthless, unknown villain ; her child, her Edward, in the hands of a desperate band of sea-robbers and smugglers ; her infant daughter, the sweet and helpless Lettie, left alone in the care of her faithful nurse.

Poor Judith ! When she found that her mistress was borne beyond her reach, she stood for a moment in speechless agony ; then turning with many and loud lamentations, she sought the cottage of Mrs. Bowline, there to tell her tale of desolation and wo.

And the boy—the blue-eyed Edward, where was he ?

When the boat of the smugglers shoved off from the Prescott, after leaving the red-haired stranger and his victim on board, they rowed swiftly up the bay, and in an unfrequented old dock near the mouth of Charles river, made a landing. Their leader, the hang-

(7)

man and villanous looking fellow, whom we have already named, Champ, took up the muffled form of the boy, which, until now, had been lying in the bottom of the boat, and while the others fastened the boat, removed a part of the bandage, so as to permit the poor little fellow to breathe a little more freely, for he had been almost stifled.

"What are you agoin' to do with the younker, Cap'n ?" asked one of the boat's crew as he turned from the pile to which he had knotted the boat's fastening.

"Why, the devil take me, if I know ! I've a mind to keep him myself."

"We had all a hand in speakin' for the lad's life!" exclaimed another: "I don't see why we haven't all a right to him. He ought to belong to the gang as much as the boat does !"

"Well! well! we'll see about it when we get to the crib : so heave ahead, lads, we've got the chink, and we'll have a blow-out to-night!" responded the leader, and in a moment more they were rapidly passing through the narrow and dark street, toward their rendezvous.

At the same moment the noble ship Prescott was standing out through Nantasket Roads to sea, with her canvass bellying to the fresh, westerly breeze. Her captain little dreamed that his last female passenger was other than the stranger's sick sister ; little indeed did he think that Mrs. Edmiston was a prisoner on board of his own ship.

We have now accounted for three of the ill-fated family ; but the fourth, whom we left at sea in the straits of Sunda, off the Isle of Java, must not be forgotten.

He, too, had a part to perform on this eventful night, and singular was the coincidence.

The sun was sinking behind the hills to the westward of Batavia-bay, and its bright, parting rays fell softly along the still waters of the harbour, which, with its twenty beautiful islands, looked like a choice bit of a lovely sky, dotted over with the soft fleecy clouds of summer. There were many vessels in the harbour, and amongst these loomed up the tall masts of the ship Ruth, and almost within the reach of the shadows which fell beyond her masts, lay a magnificent English frigate, sleeping quietly at anchor, as if never "like a thing of life," had she battled with the tempest and played with the gale.

When the sun was about an half hour above its time of setting, a boat pushed from the side of the Ruth and pulled rapidly away towards the beautiful Isle of Alkmar, which lies in the outer edge of the harbour. There were but two persons in the boat, besides the crew at the oars. One was Captain Edmiston ; the other was Frank Darlington. The first was seated in sad silence, apparently in deep meditation ; the other frequently and anxiously glanced toward the frigate, which lay so quietly on the calm bosom of the glittering bay.

Soon the boat reached the green shores of the beautiful island. Captain Edmiston and Mr. Darlington landed, while the seamen drew the boat upon the glittering strand.

"It seems to me that Hawkhurst is rather tardy, especially when we consider that this invitation is from him!" remarked Edmiston with a languid smile, as he again glanced toward the frigate.

"The hour was to be sunset, and some twenty minutes must elapse before then," answered the other; and then again glancing toward the frigate, from which a boat was now pushing off, he added, "he will be here in time!"

"It is well; you have a full knowledge of my wishes, and to your judgment and action I entrust myself and my honour. I will retire to yon little hillock until you settle the preliminaries with his second," said Edmiston, and proceeding to the spot which he designated, he calmly and carelessly reclined upon the sod, collecting at the same time a bouquet of wild flowers which were growing within his reach, and arranging them as tastefully as if he was about to present them to the idol of his love.

Meantime the boat from the English frigate rapidly approached the island. In the stern sheets sat three officers, one of whom the reader may recognise as Lord Hawkhurst.

As they landed, Darlington advanced to meet them, and was received by Lord Hawkhurst with a cold, haughty bow, but rather more politely by the second person, who wore the uniform of a lieutenant, and who had probably before conferred with Mr. Darlington, as he now addressed him by name.

"It is near the time, Mr. Darlington," said he, "and we had better at once settle the preliminaries. We have brought both pistols and swords, and, in case of necessity, we have brought our ship's surgeon along."

"There must be no need of a surgeon, sir," said Hawkhurst, bitterly. "I come here not to play—it is his life or mine, or both!"

"I regret such a bitter and deadly determination!" said the English lieutenant to Darlington, apologetically; "but let me know your weapons. You have the right of choice, being the challenged party."

"Pistols, sir!" answered the American.

"And your distance?" asked the other.

"Twelve paces," was the reply.

"Too distant! Rather place us breast to breast;" exclaimed Hawkhurst, angrily."

"Excuse me, Lord Hawkhurst; but our right, as the challenged party, gives us the choice of distance as well as weapons," answered Darlington, firmly.

"Very well, sir; have it all your own way, but bear a hand about it! I am in no mood for dallying."

"Nor are we, sir; but I prefer to confer with your second."

"Well, sir," replied the latter, "we need not confer long. I pre-

sume you will let your principal use one of our pistols; we have a
very fine case here of Manton's make."

" Thank you," replied Darlington, " Captain Edmiston has a
favourite pair, which he has used before, and as they have been
lucky, he will prefer to use them on this occasion. His Lordship
may recognise them !"

" Sir, I came here to fight your friend, not to be insulted by
you !" angrily retorted Hawkhurst, who was evidently galled by
the pointed allusion.

" Very well, sir, you shall not be disappointed," was the reply
of Darlington, who was purposely irritating the opponent of his
friend in order to render him nervous, and if possible to disconcert
him and render his hand unsteady, for he well knew that Lord
Hawkhurst had long been preparing for this meeting, and feared the
worst for his friend.

The two seconds now retired a short distance to measure off
the ground; while the surgeon selected a smooth grass plat where
he seated himself, and, opening his case of instruments, commenced a cool examination of them, taking his pocket handkerchief
out, and wiping the bright steel as if already certain of the necessity for their use.

Meantime, Lord Hawkhurst paced nervously up and down the
beach, casting frequent glances toward him who reclined so calmly
upon the knoll beyond, with the wild flowers which he had gathered
in his hand.

At last the ground was measured, a pistol from each party's case
selected and carefully charged, and then the seconds each sought
their principal.

" We are ready now, Captain Edmiston," said Darlington, as he
approached his friend; and then, as his voice trembled, he added,
" have you any further orders in case of an unfortunate termination
to this meeting ?"

" Yes, if I fall, give my poor wife these flowers, and tell her that
while I gathered them, I thought alone of her and my sweet babies,
whom the holy God of Heaven protect. My will is made ; you are
its executor."

" Come, sir, we are all ready," said Hawkhurst's second, approaching Darlington : " let us place our men."

Then the two foes walked steadily to the selected spot, and each
stopped at the spot marked by his second. Oh ! it was a strange,
a sad sight to see those two men, formed in nature's noblest mould,
standing there with the frown of deadly hatred gathered on their
brows, prepared each to shed the other's blood.

The seconds now drew lots to see which should give the word.
It fell to the second of Hawkhurst.

" Give it slow !" said the latter, bitterly : " I want time !"

The pistols were now placed in the hands of the foes ; the seconds
withdrew from the line of fire ; and then the usual inquiry was
made :

" Are you ready, gentlemen ?"

" I am," was the low, firm reply of Edmiston.

" Yes, !" was the short, fierce-toned answer of Hawkhurst.

Then came the fearful words :

"One, two, three ! fire !" and almost at the same instant followed the reports of both pistols.

The seconds rushed to their principals, both of whom stood calm and uninjured. Both had fired too hurriedly for a deadly aim, for the second of Lord Hawkhurst had disobeyed his principal's request in giving the word, and had purposely given it quickly.

" Curses on such fighting," angrily exclaimed Hawkhurst ; and then turning to Edmiston, he added, " If you, sir, are as anxious to settle this matter as I am, you will prefer weapons which are more sure ! Rapiers are lying in yonder boat !"

" I will not balk your desires, Lord Hawkhurst !" was the calm reply of the other.

" Bring me the swords !" shouted the excited Lord to one of his boat's crew ; and in a moment a pair of rapiers were handed to him by the seamen.

" They are of equal length," said he, contemptuously tossing one toward his antagonist.

The latter raised the weapon, and bent the bright blade in his hand, as if to test its temper, and then threw himself into position and awaited the attack.

The next moment their blades were crossed. Lord Hawkhurst was a most skilful swordsman, and now pushed his attack with much more calmness and self-possession than his manner at the commencement promised. Edmiston was equally calm, and, though evidently not so practised at his weapon, had a decided advantage over his opponent, as he stood entirely on the defensive. For a few minutes Hawkhurst put in his lunges steadily and rapidly, but each was met and parried skilfully by his opponent ; and then the young Lord's excitable nature began to warm up, and swifter and more deadly were his lunges. These of course left him more exposed, and twice had Edmiston's weapon returned his thrusts, each time slightly wounding him, when the left foot of Captain Edmiston, who was at the moment pressing forward upon his antagonist, caught in a vine which lay concealed in the long green grass over which they were trampling, and the unfortunate man stumbled forward and was received upon the keen point of his adversary's weapon, which, even up to its silver hilt, was passed through his shoulder.

With a shout of triumphant exultation, Hawkhurst drew forth his blood-stained weapon from the fearful wound.

" Oh, holy heaven, my poor wife !" faintly uttered the wounded man, as he tottered forward into the arms of his second.

" What message shall I bear to her ? She is in England before now, awaiting my return !" said Hawkhurst, with a smile of fiendish glee, as he bent over his victim.

" Great God protect her !" moaned poor Edmiston, as the dreadful truth seemed to strike his mind ; and then he beckoned his enemy to come nearer, and in a low, deep tone added—" Hawkhurst, for the love of the mother who bore you, for the sake of the Almighty God who made you, do not harm my helpless wife and babes ! You probably have taken my life; let that satisfy your revenge."

" It is but a drop in the bucket !" hissed the fiendish enemy. " *She*, your Roxanna, awaits my return to England."

" The curse of Almighty God rest upon you, and sink your fiendish soul below the lava waves of hell itself if you do aught to harm that sweet angel !" cried Edmiston, with the energy of that despair, which is too deep and strong for our weak pen to describe.

" ' *That angel* ' shall find her heaven in my arms, and—"

" Bloody fiend of hell, add not insult to this infernal work !" cried Darlington, as he dashed the insulting Lord away from the form of his victim, with one powerful motion of his strong arm.

" By Jupiter ! I'll place you beside him !" shouted the infuriated Lord, springing to regain his weapon.

" No, my Lord, this must not be !" interposed the lieutenant, withholding the weapon.   " One victim surely is enough !"

" Enough for the present, but there are *three* more !" bitterly exclaimed the baffled man, as he saw the imploring eyes of his suffering antagonist fixed upon him.

" Is there no hope ?" asked Darlington of the surgeon who had been examining the wound.

" I fear but little," was the sad answer : " he cannot live five minutes if the hemorrhage is internal."

" Darlington, hasten home—protect my wife and children—here, the flowers !" faintly whispered the wounded man, as he drew from his blood-stained bosom, the bouquet of wild flowers, which he had gathered before the combat commenced.

" I will ! I will ! so help me, God !" exclaimed the unhappy friend, " if indeed you are to die ; but there yet is hope, this gush of blood may be stanched. You will aid me, will you not, sir ?"

" I will," replied the surgeon, and at once proceeded to his duties, but was angrily told to desist by Hawkhurst, who ordered him into the boat.

" For the sake of common humanity, sir, permit me to do my duty as a man to a fellow being in suffering !" said the surgeon.

" Sir, bandy no words with me ; you are under my orders, and I now command you to leave that cursed dog to his fate, and to go on board of the frigate at once !"

" You may yet have need of his services, Lord Hawkhurst ; there is a little daylight left, which I am desirious to improve, and I now demand *immediate satisfaction* for this insulting and unmanly course toward my wounded friend !" cried Darlington, now completely aroused by the brutal conduct of Lord Hawkhurst.

"And who are you, pray, who dares to talk to me of satisfaction?" sneeringly asked the latter.

"A man, sir; a better than yourself, and this shall be proved to you before many minutes pass!"

"How—upstart?"

"Choose your weapons, and learn, sir!"

"By Heaven, I've a mind to humour ye in your desire to be laid alongside of your groaning master."

"Take your weapon, sir, ere my forbearance is driven to that pitch which will urge me to strike you while unarmed! Now!" cried Darlington, as he took one of the swords and tossed the other to Hawkhurst.

The young lord seized the weapon, and with angry curses advanced to the attack. Meantime, the surgeon was engaged in endeavouring to stanch and bandage the wound of Edmiston, and though the Lieutenant was engaged in narrowly watching the combatants, to see that no unfair means were used, the doctor was so intent on his humane duty that the quick clashing of the weapons, the panting of the excited men, and their rapid, heavy steps, did not even cause him to raise his head, until a loud cry from Hawkhurst startled him, just as he had finished putting on his last application of lint.

"Curse ye! curse ye! why was I tempted to fight you, when I was already weak with loss of blood!" cried Hawkhurst, as he staggered forward, and fell upon the sod, while the hot blood gushed from a wound in nearly a similar place to that of Edmiston's.

"You had best help your commander, sir," said Darlington to the surgeon; "if my hand has been as steady and true as my intention, he is in the same state of danger that my poor friend is!"

"I hope not worse!" said the surgeon, as he hastened to the side of the fallen man; "for your friend may recover, with proper care. I think that no main artery is injured!"

"*He live!* Oh, God! then let me live once more to meet him!" faintly uttered Hawkhurst.

The night shadows were now gathering upon the waters, and as soon as the surgeon could prepare them to be removed, both of the wounded men were removed to their boats, and thence to their respective vessels.

Edmiston was too faint with loss of blood to speak, as he was borne into his cabin on board the Ruth, but Darlington knew his duty too well to require orders, and he at once hastened the relading of the ship; for he, too, with Edmiston, had feared the worst for the helpless ones at home, when he recollected the strange taunts of Hawkhurst in the moment of his first victory.

Therefore ten days only had elapsed before the ship Ruth was standing out of the harbour, homeward bound, with every sail set which could draw.

A few moments before her anchor had been hove up to her bows, the kind English surgeon, who had proved as skilful as he was humane, paid his last visit to the ship.

"I have to thank you for your noble kindness," said Darlington to him, as they stood at the gangway, beside which his boat was waiting, "but Captain Edmiston desires me to hand you this token of his esteem and gratitude. This purse contains twenty pounds——"

"Not a penny! not a penny will I take for doing simply my duty in this case!" exclaimed the warm-hearted Englishman. "Not a penny—but do you take good care to keep his wound open till he gets out of this rascally hot climate. Were it to close, it would mortify."

"I will obey your orders, doctor, but you must accept——"

"Not a penny!"

"Well, sir, if you will not accept *his* money, you cannot refuse this token of *my* gratitude and esteem!" said Darlington, taking a beautiful gold watch from his pocket, and detaching from it a safety guard made of dark glossy hair, at the same time adding—— "Excuse me for taking off the guard, but it is a precious thing to me; it was taken from above the fair brow of one of the noblest girls that ever hove an anchor into a man's heart, braided by herself, and of course——"

"You shouldn't part with it! But I accept your watch, my noble friend, on condition that you take this ring and wear it, and whenever you or any of your friends call upon Blount Hazlewood if he denies them heart, hand, or purse, or the aid of all and either, then the devil take him, that's all!"

"Thank you, my kind friend; thank you! This interchange of gifts will serve to keep our memory alive. We met unpleasantly, yet not so do we part."

"No, I could almost say that I'm glad everything has happened just as it has. Every time I glance at this watch, I shall remember you, the hour of sunset, and this moment!"

Darlington glanced at the massive gold ring which had been placed on his finger. It had a large cornelian set, on which was engraved a cross, as the emblem of faith and truth, an anchor, as the emblem of hope and resolution, and a pierced heart as the emblem of love.

"And I shall never forget Blount Hazlewood!" said he, in return. One warm grasp of the hand and the friends had parted, perhaps for ever.

The English officer returned to his vessel to attend to his titled patient, who was still in a critical condition, which was rendered even more dangerous by his excitable and ungovernable temper. The Ruth was under way within ten minutes after Doctor Hazlewood had left her deck, and she was homeward bound.

CHAPTER XIV.

Ho for the King of the sea!
Ho for the fearless and free!
Ho for the ocean so blue!
Ho for the sea-king's crew!
Ho for the battle's wild strife!
Ho for the Rover's mad life!
  Ashore or afloat,
  On land or in boat,
Ho for the King of the sea!
Ho for the fearless and free!

NEVER was a wilder, never a scene more grandly picturesque!

On the northern end of the island of Madagascar, near where the many islets of the Comora group cluster in their evergreen beauty, in the Mozambique channel, at a point encircled by a group of small and nameless islands, there is a cove or small bay which is entirely shut in from the sea, being only approachable through a narrow island-channel, which was so full of coral reefs that none but an experienced pilot could safely guide a vessel through its intricate windings. At the head of this bay was a small

(8)

area of level ground, which was scatteringly grown over with tall trees, and sodded with grass and flowers; but inland it was entirely surrounded by lofty and rugged precipices, which reared their rough and impassable fronts on all sides save where the waves of the bay rippled against the strand. Down the sides of these rugged pre cipices little rivulets leaped in foamy brightness, and after reaching the level meadow below, meandered through the grass and flowers in little silvery threads down to the bay, which was formed by the group of islands already alluded to and a triangular indentation in the land. The level spot, which might contain twenty or more acres, was a perfect Eden. It was almost entirely overshadowed by tall and beautiful trees; there was no rough and ungainly under-growth, but beneath the out-spreading limbs of the grove was a level sward of rich green grass, profusely strewn with flowers, except in portions which had been trodden down by the feet of the inhabitants.

It is time we alluded to the latter, but let us first describe the appearance of the bay.

Nearly in its centre lay a tall and rakish brig of about two hundred tons measurement; a vessel built with the long, low hull, sharp, flaring bows, broad beam and tapering run, which has ever made Baltimore-built crafts famous. The brig was indeed a clipper. Her immensely heavy spars raked entirely over her stern, and from the tall peak of her main sky-sail-mast hung a flag, which, as the breeze swung open its folds, revealed her character. It was a magnificent banner, the body of it composed of crimson silk, upon which was embroidered in blue and gold; a figure at once noble and commanding, standing upon the foamy waves of the ocean, crowned with a wreath of coral and shells, bearing in his hand a flowing flag with "The King of the Sea," worked in golden letters therein. So lifelike was the embroidery upon this banner, that it seemed like a living figure when it floated lazily out upon the breeze.

The vessel was evidently fitted for warlike service. Two long brass thirty-two pounder pivot-guns were upon her deck; around her masts, racks of glittering boarding pikes were arranged; rows of brass-hilted cutlasses fringed the trunk of the after cabin. There were but few men about her decks, and these were all armed with pistols and cutlasses.

Nearer the shore lay several smaller vessels, each wearing a red flag with the emblem of crossed swords thereon; but none save the beautiful brig wore the banner of *the King of the Sea.* Yet the counterpart of that banner was waving in the same breeze.

On shore, on the inner edge of the triangular space, immediately at the foot of the rugged precipice which surrounded it, ranged a row of neatly-built cottages. In front of each, and around it, was a small garden-plat, containing flowers and vegetables. In the centre of this range of houses was a larger and more ornamental building than the others, and from a flag-staff in front of this house, waved a rich flag similar ✿ that which floated from the mast-head of the brig.

The buildings, which were twenty or thirty in number, were all inhabited, as appeared by the men, women and children in the vicinity, who were coming and going to and fro. Some of the latter were gambolling and racing over the green-sward which lay between the cottages and the bay; others were wading in the crystal rivulets which lazily meandered through the meadow, gathering the bright flowers which grew along the banks, or picking up from the pebbly beds bright stones and little shells.

The men and women were scattered about, some reclining under the shady trees, others seated in their door-ways, and others wandering along the margin of the bay. All of the men were armed, and all wore a uniform of blue and white, trimmed richly with gold.

Never was a scene more wildly picturesque than this to which we introduce the reader. The place, the singular flags, the armed men and vessels, all denoted it to be a rendezvous of pirates; yet the women and children, so peaceful and apparently happy, seemed to contradict the usual habits of the lawless, unloving, undomesticated robbers of the sea.

Yet the reader will not wonder when we inform him that the females were nearly all Malays and Indians, and though tawny and dusky in hue, were of fine and noble figures. The men seemed to be composed of all nations. The dark and fiery Malay, the fair but portly Englishman, the haughty and impetuous Spaniard, were there, amid Americans, French, and Italians. It was indeed a strange and motley crew.

Amongst the women an occasional one might be seen of skin more fair, and azure eye, denoting her European derivation; but they were very few.

The location, so near the channel and track of the East India-men, seemed admirably adapted to their purpose. It was well secured for defence, and at the same time well hidden by the inland hills and the lofty islands to seaward.

At the time to which we introduce the reader to this scene, a summer day in 1845, there was a strange scene occurring in the larger of the buildings, which was designated by the flag-staff and banner as the residence of the chief.

A man lay upon a couch in the last agony of life, and judging from the splendour of the apartment and the state which surrounded him he was none other than their chief. His eyes were as black as the clouds of night, and his pale, clammy brow was overhung with masses of hair, which was but partly gray, while the beard and moustache which completely covered the lower part of his face was as jetty as the raven's spotless wing, and coarse as the un-combed mane of a wild horse. His features were quite rude and repulsive, but his face seemed thin and haggard with suffering. It was covered over with scars, and though now pale and bloodless, yet showed the marks of a weather-beaten life. He seemed to be at least fifty years of age, and as he lay uncovered upon the rich couch, his form seemed to have been of Herculean strength before it had been shrunken by the touch of sickness.

Those around him were richly dressed, by their arms and appearance seeming to be the officers of the band.

One of these, who stood nearest the side of the chief, demands a passing notice from the reader. He was a young athletic person, whose light brown hair, blue eyes, and fair complexion, contrasted strangely with the dark-hued men around him. His dress, though plainer in appearance, was richer in material and more neat in its fit than the garb of the others, and his weapons were of a choicer kind.

In sad silence he bent over the couch of the chief, his manner expressing the deepest concern and pity. He did not look to be over twenty-four, or twenty-five years of age, yet his full and muscular form, his firm and thoughtful countenance, his air of resolution and command, might have betokened more years.

" Raise me up, Bertram," said the occupant of the couch, faintly, to the youth. " I have a yarn to spin before I slip my moorings."

The young man obeyed the request.

Then the chief in feeble tones addressed the persons who stood before him. " I have sent for ye, gentlemen, because I find that I've taken my last cruise with ye, and you will shortly have to sail under other orders than mine. It is necessary for me to choose a successor, and to leave ye a few orders regarding the disposition of this worn-out hull of mine !"

" Your will shall be obeyed !" responded each and all.

" Ay, even as it ever has been !" said the dying chief, and for a moment the fire of proud command gleamed from his fast-dimming eye ; and then he added, " Draw ye closer around me, and hear my last orders." Then did those wild, strange-looking men crowd closer to the couch of their chief, who continued his words : " Whom would ye now choose for your king? whom will ye have for a leader ?" There was no answer, but each one glanced at the other, as if unknowing whom to choose. " He should be the bravest among ye," continued the pirate.

" Ay—let the choice be thine !" answered the officers of the band.

" Bertram, stand forth !" responded the chief ; and then as he glanced towards his officers, he exclaimed, " Here is my choice ! Not that he is a boy of my own rearing ; not because he is the son of my adoption ; but because he hath proved himself *fit !* Hath he not ?"

" Ay, ay ! let Bertram be our king !" was the universal response.

" That, then, is settled. Now hear more. Bury me not in the earth, where the flesh-worms may feed upon my body ; but take my corpse aboard the brig, and bear it out into blue water, and wrapping it up in my old flag, ballast it with gold—ay, with the red gold of my own winning, and let it sink with its golden drapery down into the blue depths of the everlasting waters. Ay, bury me in state; let martial music sound over the waters; let the loud cannon shake the rolling waves with the music I have loved all my life! Bury me as I have lived; bury me like a KING OF THE SEA!"

"It shall be done!" responded each and all of the band.

"It is well! I shall die now as I have lived—contented and like a man! Leave me, all, save Bertram. You may stay, boy, for I have much to say to ye, and but little space to speak it in. And now, comrades, ye must now take a parting grip of this hand which so long has served ye. Be ye as true to Bertram as ye have been to me; be as true to him as my sword which I leave to him has been to its owner, and I will pledge my dying word that he'll prove worthy of your trust!"

One by one those lawless men advanced to the side of their chief, and for the last time clasped the cold hand of their dying leader. It was strange to see the big tears steal down their rough, dark, scarred cheeks; yet they, who better loved the battle and the tempest than tender lover loves his lady's voice and song—they, stern and cold as they seemed, wept! And as they shook his weak and pulseless hand, one by one, with heavy sighs they turned away, and soon he was left alone with the youth whom he had called Bertram, his chosen successor.

"Boy!" cried the dying chief, in a faint but kind tone, "boy, I've a duty to do by ye before I die, one which I mayhap have too long neglected. You have been reared by me in what the world might call a bad way. It has been at all rates a bold and free one. You have often asked who you were, knowing that you were but my adopted son."

"Yes, yes!" eagerly exclaimed the young man; "for the love of heaven tell me who and what I am! My father! My mother!"

"I don't know who they are, boy, exactly; but your father was an English lord, or a lord's son, I hardly know which; but do you open yon locker in the corner to starboard of the door, and bring me a package rolled up in canvass which you'll find there!" The young man obeyed the order, and finding the designated package brought it to the couch. "Unlash it!" said the chief.

This too was done, and when it was opened, the young man saw a suit of child's apparel, and a gold-cased miniature, a likeness of a man dressed in the uniform of an officer.

"What means this? Whose is this portrait? It looks strangely like mine own face, only much older!"

"I expect it is your father, boy. It was slung around your neck by that same braid of dark brown hair, when I first saw ye!"

"When and how was that? Oh, tell me who and what I am!"

"You are now the KING OF THE SEA, boy! You were, when I first saw ye, a helpless infant."

"My father and mother?"

"I don't know anything about *him,* but your mother was a sweet, fair creature, when I saw her for the first and last time; but she was in a bad fix, and I, like a cursed rascal, helped to get her in it!"

"For the love of heaven, explain! This suspense is too much!"

"Boy, I can't—it's a hard yarn for me to spin, and I'm getting weak very fast. But I've made an entry in my private log-book, which you may read after I'm put under blue water. It may tell ye more than ye wish to know, both of your history and mine own; for mark ye, boy, you are now the King of the Sea, the chief of mine own band, and were ye King of England ye could not leave them! I know you were born to better things, but I saved your life, and now I give you mine own heritage. What can I more?"

"Nothing; oh, nothing. But this portrait, it *must* be my father, it is so like to me!"

"Ay, boy, 'tis like, it is; but twenty-two or three years have passed since you have seen father or mother, and now they may be dead, and you left alone in the world—no, not alone, with all our braves at your will!"

"I would like to know if they live."

"Who, boy?"

"Why, my father and mother!"

"Nonsense, youngster; if they do, you have long since been forgotten."

"Never—never, if they live! A parent's love is not fragile as the mists of the morning, or even as the snow in the warm spring-time!"

"Well, well, boy, I'll not contradict you. I'm weakening fast. Do you read that will which I've left in my log-book, when I've slipped life's rusty cable, and obey my last requests!"

"I will, I will!" said Bertram, with deep feeling.

One hour later, and Robert Champ, the long-dreaded, and but too well known pirate of the Mozambique Channel—the fearless "KING OF THE SEA"—was a cold motionless corpse.

CHAPTER XV.

There is a ship on the sea,
And stormy its path,
For the tempest it moveth
In power and wrath;
There's a woman in peril,
But rescue is near,
When the darkest her danger,
The deepest her fear;
And the long-parted have met,
But absent is one,
And the mother yet weepeth
The loss of her son!

READER, appreciating your anxiety to know the fate of poor Mrs. Edmiston, we devote this chapter to a retrospective glance in that direction.

The fresh westerly breeze which filled the sails of the Prescott, when she stood out of Boston harbour, on the night when the unhappy lady was abducted, was but the priming to the load which was to follow it. She passed Cape Ann light with her top-gallant sails set; but, ere long, her bending spars creaked the sailors' warning, and sail after sail was taken in or reduced by reefs, so that the next morning's light found her scudding under her close-reefed-topsails, bounding over the foaming waves, like a fear-chased thing of real life; neither land nor sail in sight; nought but rushing clouds above; nought but foaming water below; nought but the wild, moaning winds around.

Oh! it is a grand sight to see a ship's vast hull cleave through the foamy surges; now, plunging down into the cavern-like hollows of the mighty rollers, then, standing on their very crests, like a lone tree on a hill-top. Ay, it is grand, but yet, 'tis fearful.

On before the heavy western gale sped the Prescott; on, like a a bird that flieth towards its nest. Her officers and crew were fearless, for the sea was regular; their masts and tackling well-rigged and fitted, their ship in order—they did not dream that danger was near. On, through the course of the first day, swiftly, but safely, dashed the noble ship. And then, when night came on, the wind began to lull a little; but this, and the general appearance of the weather, indicated not the end of the storm, but a shift in the direction of the wind.

The sea rolled very high, yet as long as it and the wind rolled from the westward, the ship could keep her course, and every hour gave her a better offing. Midnight came on and with it a dead calm. There was something awful in the sudden cessation of the wind, and the dense darkness which accompanied it. The sea rolled on as high and as wild before, but the foam melted away as the wind went down, like snow before a summer's sun. A now, above, below, around, was dark, fearfully dark, ominously quiet.

For some moments the ship lay heaving upon the seas, her reefed sails flapping against the yards and masts, not even having steerage way upon her.

Captain Bowline had stationed all hands at the braces, ready to trim the yards, when the wind again struck the ship, and was now standing beside his helmsman, watching with deep anxiety for the first gust which might come; for he knew that to be struck aback in a sea so heavy would be fearfully dangerous. Still a few moments more and no sign of the direction from whence it would come, though all knew that the awful calm would soon be broken.

Suddenly, as if from the bosom of the heaving ocean, came a long, deep, unearthly moan. It swept across the waters and through the thick air like the voice of some living monster in agony. When Bowline heard it, he cast one anxious glance all around the the horizon as if to see whence it came; but it had seemed to fill the whole air—he knew not which way to brace his yards to meet the dreadful gale, which he now knew would soon break upon him. Again came that fearful storm-groan, and the air seemed to tremble out an answer to it. Ned Brace, the chief mate, stood by the Captain's side, and when for the third time that deep thrilling sound crept through the air and over the dark heaving waters, the face of the bold seaman turned as pale as the canvass which flapped above his head.

"Cap'n Bowlin'!" said he; "I never heard that but once before, and then—"

"To the braces! Bear a hand, men! Clear away larboard, haul in to starboard!" shouted Bowline, interrupting the yarn his mate was about to spin. It was time indeed to brace in, for while that last fearful sound was rolling off along the distant waters, the whole range of clouds in the north-east was lit up with one long, red, ragged flash of lightning; then came a peal as if the very magazines of thunder had blown up; and down toward the ship, like a moving mountain of cloud, and foam, and spray, swept the storm, bearing full upon her larboard bow. "Stand by the halliards and sheets! Let go all! It'll sweep the sticks out of her, if there's a thread of sail set!" again shouted Bowline, as he saw with what fearful force the wind came on.

But ere the order was passed from his lips, the gale was upon them. The ship received the tornado on her bow, and as it struck her close-reefed topsails, she seemed to press down into the water to leeward as if the weight of a mountain was setting upon her. Down, down, she careened, her masts bent like reeds in a hurricane, her lee-yard arms were down to the water's edge, she moved not a foot ahead, she seemed to be slowly descending into the dark abyss of the ocean, while that awful gale roared over her trembling hull, and through her strained masts.

"Cut away sheets and halliards, and stand by to clear her of her top-hamper!" shouted Bowline through his trumpet. But little hope was there of a human voice being heard in such a gale, which now saved all trouble of cutting away, for the bending spars and strained canvass, unable to bear the fearful weight of the gale, snapped and burst from all fastenings, and in one moment more, the ship was stripped of spars, canvass, and all! Nothing but her lower masts were left standing. And, as eased from this load, she righted a little, her bows veered off before the wind, and then with the wreck of her masts and yards and the flying strips of her torn sails clanging about in the gale, she dashed off before the wind.

The sea, now crossed by the gale, pitched and jumped in huge and fearful waves, one crossing the other, now boarding on one side and then on the other.

All hands were at work clearing the wreck of spars away, at one moment half buried in the foam and spray, as the ship plunged into the water; the next lifted high on the very peak of black surges.

Captain Bowline stood clinging to the mizzen-rigging, from time to time giving orders to the helmsman with his trumpet, as he saw the seas sweep down upon the strained vessel. At this terrible moment, when the vessel seemed as if she would split asunder, when there seemed no hope of safety even to the brave seamen,

(9)

Bowline saw the red-haired stranger creep upon deck—terror written in his pale face.

Trembling, he crept across the deck till he reached the rigging where the brave Captain had fixed himself. There, pale and shuddering, he clung like a base helpless craven, as he looked.

"Why do you leave your poor sister at a time like this, sir?" said the Captain, angrily.

"Is there—much—danger?" replied the wretch, half choked with his terror.

"Why don't you stay below and take care of your sister, I say? We want no land-lubbers up here in the way!" again shouted the Captain.

"O, Captain, save me; I'm not fit to die!" moaned the wretch, as if his life was in the hands of mere man.

At the same instant, even above the roar of the gale, even above the dash of the sea, came the sound of a piercing shriek from the cabin.

Then even paler turned that villain's face, and half unconsciously he muttered, "O Lord, I'm lost! She's got the muffler off from her mouth."

At the same instant the negro cabin steward, who for the last five years had sailed in the same ship, rushed up from below, and while the white of his big eyes rolled to and fro in wonder and fear, he shouted to the Captain—

"O, Massa Cap'n! O, Massa Cap'n Bowline! Dere's a ghostess down below! I've seen her scream; an' I've hearn her face, and it's jist all the same as Missy Edmisson!"

"Curses on your head, you black scoundrel!" shouted the red-haired stranger; "it is not her—I never—" and as he sprung from the rigging towards the negro, the villain slipped and fell upon deck. At the same instant a sea swept on board, for a moment drenching him and completely hiding him from view as it dashed him against the inside of the opposite bulwarks. When he again arose, there was indeed a transmogrification in his appearance. His head, which a moment before was covered with long, bushy, red hair, was now as bare as the deck below him; his chin and face which had been covered with a shaggy pair of whiskers, was smooth and beardless. The sea, or his fall, had broken the fastenings of his wig and false beard, and he now stood uncovered in his villany.

"I'm out in my reckoning if there ain't something wrong agoin' on here. You said you saw a ghost down below, that looked just like Mrs. Edmiston, Jake?"

"Yes, Massa Cap'n, I did see a ghostess, an' I hear hum holler, and it was jist all same as Missy Edmisson!"

"Here, Mr. Brace," shouted the Captain; "look out for the vessel! I'm going below a minute to unreeve this 'ere mystery. There's some foul work agoin' on here. Look ye, you man there, that's been sailin' under false colours, do you stay on deck till I

come up agin! I don't like to see men afeard to show the colour
o' their hair and the cut o' their jib. Mr. Brace, keep an eye on
that chap; he's cared so little for that poor sister o' his in this 'ere
bad fix that we've been in, that I think I'd better see if she don't
want something."

As the Captain said this, he turned to go below, first handing
his trumpet to Mr. Brace, who had come aft to relieve him in the
watch; but the wigless, hairless stranger rushed to the companion-
way, at the same time, crying—

"Oh, don't try to see her, Captain! I can take care of her! I
was frightened a little—but I ain't now."

"Stay on deck, sir, stay on deck till I come up again, I tell ye!
I'm captain here, and I don't like the cut of your jib, now that you
are stripped to your bare poles—I don't."

The man, who was indeed under a " *bare poll,*" fell back before the
stern and menacing manner of the Captain, who now descended
into the cabin. Meantime, on, on, madly, swiftly, wildly, before the
tempest, scudded the ship.

When the Captain went below, the stranger, whose anxiety
seemed now to have risen above his fear, started to follow him, but
his first step was arrested by Brace, who shouted—

"Avast there, you half-drowned specimen of a land shark! Take
another step towards that companion-way and I'll make fish-bait of
ye!"

The man paused, then turned toward the lee mizen rigging, up
which he scrambled two or three ratlines high and then clung there,
trembling, and waited the re-appearance of Captain Bowline. He
had not long to wait, for in a few moments that worthy's head was
seen hastily rising above the cabin hatchway, and though Captain
Bowline's face usually had plenty of colour in it, never had Ned
Brace or anybody else seen it so red before.

"Oh, you villanous thief!" shouted he, looking at the wigless one,
who now clambered a little higher up the rigging. "Oh, you low-
lived land swab! I've seen your sister. Oh, you hell-hound!
Come down out o' that. Mr. Brace, get some spare rigging in your
hand, I mean to tow that fellow into port—for he shall sail no
longer in this ship! Oh, you nigger, come down out o' that rig-
gin'!" But the wretch, instead of coming down, still clambered
higher, and was now clinging to the shrouds, under the top-rim, and
as he paused here, he begged for mercy. "Oh, yes; you'd like to
take care of your poor sister, wouldn't ye? Now do you jist come
down from aloft there, before I send up after ye!" shouted the enraged Captain; then turning to Brace, he added. "Who do you
think that rascal's poor crazy sister is, Mr. Brace?"

"Why I haven't the remotest idea, Cap'n, only I think that he's
a lying shark, that's all."

"Well, Brace, it ain't nobody but our own Mrs. Edmiston, that
the infernal pirate has been tryin' to smuggle off to England for
that black-hearted Lord Hoghurst."

"What? Mrs. Edmiston? Oh, you shark! Lay down from aloft, and let me overhaul your worm-eaten log of a hull!"

"Take a hand up with you and go and help him down!" said the Captain.

To this order, Brace gave hasty obedience. The stranger was, for a landsman, in a fearful situation. He was clinging to the futtock shrouds, and as the vessel reeled to and fro in the heavy seaway, he was swinging one moment out over the black waves, the next, over the decks of the ship, and death would follow his fall in either case, if he struck inside or outside the ship. As Brace and one of the crew started up the rigging, the unhappy man attempted to crawl up over the top-rim, but just as his hands had clutched the rail that ran around the top, a heavy sea surged the ship, and his feet slipped from the futtock shrouds, and for a moment he swung helplessly in the air, clinging only with his hands. Oh, how hopeless and agonising was his downward glance as he saw that his hour had come. Again the ship surged heavily—Brace and the seaman had involuntarily paused and clung to the rigging, as they looked almost with pity on the miserable wretch. One moment more he clung with the grasp of despair to the rail, then with a yell of agony yielded to the surge; his grasp loosed, and down, down into the foaming waters with a sullen plunge he sunk. One wild cry as the ship passed on, and that was the last sound which ever reached a human ear from the lips of James Clare, alias "Lord Clarence," the tool and villain of Lord Hawkhurst.

"Saved some trouble to the hangman!" was Bowline's brief remark, as he witnessed the fate of the miserable wretch.

"That's just the sort of a man I took that ar chap to be, Cap'n Bowline, when he stood on the wharf talkin' to you and wouldn't look you in the eyes. Don't ye remember I told you then that he had bad timbers in him?"

"Ay, I do; but do you keep a look out for the barkie, Mr. Brace. I must go below and see how the poor lady gets on. We've lost so many spars, and are strained so much, that I'm agoin to run the old ship back to port for a refit. We must haul her up on a wind as soon as the wind lulls enough to get some kind o' canvass on her; keep a bright look-out, I'll be on deck again soon."

"Ay, ay, sir!" responded the mate with a very contented air, for he was thinking how well the villain who had just found a watery grave deserved his fate.

But Mr. Brace had little time to think of other things than his duty just then, for never was a good ship exposed to a worse cross sea and a heavier blow than was the Prescott on that night.

However, she weathered it, and one week afterward lay at the wharf in Boston, much to the unhappiness of the Messrs. Dibble, who were much better pleased when counting their profits than when considering their losses.

But who can imagine the agony of poor Mrs. Edmiston, when

on being landed and once more entering the door of her old home, she found but one of her sweet twins. Her darling boy had not been heard of since the dreadful moment when she had been seized by the ruthless minion of her foe, and borne on board the Prescott. Week after week was spent making vain search for some trace of the poor child; rewards were offered, but all was fruitless; and at last the mother mourned her son as dead, lost to her for ever. And sad, O, how sad was the meeting, four months afterwards, of the pale and still feeble Edmiston and his wife, when the Ruth once more dropped anchor in Boston Harbour. Yet when the twain told each to the other their trials and troubles, they gratefully knelt them down unto their Heavenly Father, and offered up a hearty thanksgiving to Him for their preservation from such dreadful dangers. And when the father, the brave, stern man, wept bitterly for his lost son, that Christian mother sadly but meekly said, " God's holy will be done! Let us not murmur. He has left us one, our own dear, dear Lettie; let us so rear and educate her that she will not only be our comfort and pride, but a blessing to the world in which God hath been pleased to place her." And then he checked the heart-dew which gushed from his sorrowing eyes, and while calmness and smiles returned to him, he kissed the blessed treasure which was linked unto his heart. No richer treasure could be given man on earth! A pure, fond, faithful, tender, sympathising, Christian wife.

CHAPTER XVI.

Oh, lay not his corse on the ground that you tread,
Where the worm grows fat on the flesh of the dead;
Oh, lay him not down in earth's burial place,
But give him a grave, where never a trace
Of the worm hath been or ever can come,
Bury him deep 'neath the old ocean's foam;
He'll fear not the shark, he'll see not the whale,
Heed not the tempest, nor care for the gale;—
Then wrap the bright flag in folds round his form,
Which waved o'er his head in battle and storm;
Let the boom of the gun be his fun'ral kuell,
Its music in life he ever loved well..
Oh, bury him thus—the King of the Sea!
Oh, bury him thus—ye fearless and free!

It was the day subsequent to the death of Robert Champ, the pirate, which we described in our fourteenth chapter. In front of the house which he had so lately occupied, the flag of the Sea-King waved from its usual staff, but it was half-mast; its counterpart at the peak of the brig at anchor in the bay was likewise half-masted, as were also the flags of the smaller proas which lay in the harbour.

The sun had just risen and shone brightly from a cloudless sky upon this beautiful spot, which we have before described. Preparations were making by the pirates to bury the chief in accordance to his last wish. The vessels were prepared for sea, and their boats had landed with a portion of their crews to bear and escort the body to the brig. It was a strange sight to see a sea-robber thus buried with all the care and ceremony which would attend the entombment of a legal king; it was strange to see a procession formed of young children dressed in white, with flower-baskets in their hands. Yet so it was ; and when at last the corpse, enveloped in one of the magnificent flags which we have described, was brought forth, borne by the chief officers of the band, headed by Bertram as chief mourner, these little children walked slowly on in front of the body to the boat, scattering flowers as they went, and chanting a low sweet song to which their little feet kept time in slow and measured steps. All this was exceeding strange, yet it showed the state of discipline and feeling to which one man, even though bold and wicked, could bring those over whom he had authority.

Robert Champ, in forming this rendezvous, had shown a knowledge of human nature, far ahead of that which has generally characterised chiefs of his profession. He knew that in having a stated and settled home for his crews, in giving them wives and homes, and drawing around them some of the domestic bonds of nature, he would keep them from a wish to separate and return to to the world, and thus had he well succeeded in forming a large and inseparable band whose interests and feelings were all centred in one spot. Fearful had the ravages of this band been upon the English East India commerce, but so intricate was the passage to their hiding-place, so well was it hidden, that not one of the many naval expeditions fitted out to find and destroy them, had yet discovered their home. They had not unfrequently given the crews and passengers of the ships which they fell in with their lives, simply taking the money and such part of the cargo as they desired ; but on some occasions, when maddened by resistance, they had indulged in the fearful and barbarous excesses which have for ever rendered the name of buccaneer infamous.

But we will return to the burial. The body of the chief was borne in solemn procession to the water-side and there placed in his own favorite barge, and then, followed by all the boats of the piratical fleet, it was taken to the brig. As it was carefully lifted over her low black bulwarks, a solemn salute of minute guns was fired, and a full band of music struck up a sweet but sorrowful funeral dirge, which rolled in soft echoes over the calm bay, which was barely rippled by a soft land-breeze. After the salute had been fired, the seamen sprang aloft, the brig's sails were loosed, and she, followed by all the smaller vessels, gracefully glided out of the harbour.

That day when the red sun stood at the meridian, the brig was hove to in blue water, in the Mozambique Channel. The other vessels were hove to close alongside of her, and while another slow and solemn salute of minute-guns was fired, the body of the Sea King, weighted down even as he had desired, with gold, instead of shot with which seamen are usually buried, was committed to the fathomless deep. No prayers were said over it; they were not men of prayer who buried him. The burial over, the vessels returned again to their anchorage and rendezvous.

It was midnight. In the same room where the pirate chief had died, sat Bertram, his successor. In his hand the young man held the miniature which had been given him by the dying chief, and which he supposed to be the likeness of his father, because it so much resembled himself. But his gaze was fixed on a journal before him; the book to which Champ in his dying moments had alluded. It was a diary of his life. One entry in this book had met the eye of Bertram, and again and again did he peruse it. As he read he murmured to himself, "O God! can it be that my father yet lives? Have I a mother—I who have never known the care of either? It is here written that I am the son of an English nobleman that I was torn from my mother's arms in my third year—I remember nothing of it, I have been with the band ever since I can recollect myself, and now if I have a father—a mother—my life and my calling will for ever bar me from them, for am I not at war with all the world? Is not all the world at war with me— and if they live, are they not of the world? This miniature was hung round my neck by this braid of dark brown hair, when I was torn from my mother's side! Where could my father then have been? He is not mentioned in connection with that event? O God! this fearful mystery is even worse than death! I know not who or what I am—ay, I *do* know that I *am* the KING OF THE SEA. I will strive to forget all else. But if this be my father, he looks like a noble man! O, that I could meet him!" The youth gazed long and ardently upon the miniature, and then hanging it by the braid around his neck, retired to his couch.

It was morning again. By order of their chief, all of the pirate band were assembled on the green before his dwelling, to receive his first orders.

There they stood, a motley band of wild, lawless, fearless men; some of them yet young and beardless, but all familiar with crime and bloodshed.

After all were assembled, the youthful leader stepped forth upon the portico which fronted the house, and as he appeared glad shouts greeted him.

"Long live Bertram the brave! Long live Bertram, the King of the Sea!"

"I thank ye for your greeting," said he, "and I now wish ye to hear my laws. Will ye abide by them?"

"Ay, we will!" was the general response.

"Then hear me! It is my will that in future no unnecessary

blood be spilled. In all cases prisoners shall be ransomed. Quarter shall always be given where it is asked. No man shall be hurt after he ceases to resist; no helpless prisoner, male or female, shall meet with abuse! These are my laws, and the first disobedience shall be punished with death! Do ye agree to this?"

"Ay, we do! Long live Bertram the brave!" shouted the band.

"It is well! I shall sail on a cruise soon. The commanders of the smaller vessels will meet me in private to receive their orders!"

What those orders were we may not know, but ere the sun had set that day, each of the proas had lifted her anchor and stood out to sea.

And on the next day the brig also made sail on a cruise, Bertram commanding her in person. It was a beautiful sight to see her, so well fitted for war, sweep out through the narrow channel; her long brass guns glittering in the sunlight; her crew, one hundred young, stout, and hearty men managing her as if she were a thing obedient to their will. When she had left the bay, all things warlike had disappeared. The women and children alone were left at the village, which in its calm and quiet beauty seemed not a nest for a pirate-horde, but some chosen spot of retirement for virtue and innocence. -

---

CHAPTER XVII.

Oh, what a changing world is this
In all things—save its wickedness!

CHANGED, oh, how changed! Reader, over twenty years have passed since we have permitted you to look in at Captain Bowline's cottage, where we left three of the Edmiston family; the parents mourning their lost son. But you might now look for the cottage, with its sweet little garden, its white walls, its green blinds, and latticed portico, with evergreen vines grown over, in vain. Where it stood, a neat row of tall brick houses are now built; its garden ground is occupied with other buildings. The rage for "improvement" has swept away its plain and rustic beauty. All things around are altered.

The favorite walk along the banks of the Mystic is no longer shaded by the grove of elms; one tree alone is left like a mourning monument of the past, upon the river's bank.

And not to Charlestown is the change confined. Go with me to Boston, and enter the counting-room where, erst time, we met the brothers Dibble. The old twin-desk is gone, there is a rich carpet on the floor, the walls, before so dark and dusty, are neatly papered over, a rich mahogany desk stands near the neatly curtained window, and before it sits, not Elihu or Samuel Dibble, but our old acquaintance, Captain Edmiston, who has succeeded them in business; they not only having retired from the same, but also from the cares of life. Samuel had died of a sudden apoplectic fit: Elihu soon followed him.

The widow of the latter had sold out to Edmiston, who, by some successful speculations in his Eastern voyages, had amassed a very considerable fortune.

There was a great change in Captain Edmiston's appearance from the time when we last saw him. His tall, erect form, was still full and powerful, but his hair was considerably turned to gray; his face was thinner and more pale; the shadows of thought, and business cares and vexations rested upon his broad, high brow.

He was not alone in the apartment. On a sofa, near a neat little stove, sat a person of full sixty years of age, if not more, a large, portly, good-humoured looking old gentleman, whose few white hairs were carefully combed athwart his bare crown, to conceal as much as possible its glossy nakedness. He had a jovial, sparkling eye, a rather red face which was filled with dimples, and though somewhat weather-beaten, still would stand very well as a sign of a hearty free-liver.

His dress was loose and comfortable, and made of the warmest material; his whole appearance indicated a man who was spending his declining days in comfort.

"I say, Edmiston?" said this elderly gentleman, "how soon'll you finish off your writin'? I'm getting rather peckish, and I've

(10)

an idea it'll be about dinner-time afore we get over home ; what d'ye say, are you a'most through ?"

" I've just finished my last letter, Bowline," replied Edmiston, " and I'm ready to go now."

" Well, heave ahead then, there's a pair of us, as the fool said to the king when he called him a knave !" responded the elderly gentleman, with a most self-satisfactory laugh, which shook his portly frame ; and both of them arose and passed from the room.

Yes, reader, this was Captain Bowline, formerly of the ship Prescott, but now retired from the perils of the sea, living on a comfortable independence, which, by prudence and economy, he had saved.   The old ship had long since been condemned as unseaworthy, and her place, as well as that of the Ruth, had been filled by a new vessel.   One of these, a magnificent ship called the Mary, was still in the East India trade, commanded by Captain Frank Darlington ; the other, a ship still larger than the Prescott, was now called the Brenda, and filled the place in the packet line which had been occupied by the former.   Both of these ships were owned by Mr. Edmiston.

We will follow him and his friend Bowline over to their home, which was in one of the brick houses which occupied the space whereon had stood Captain Bowline's old cottage.   They both still resided together, for the friendship which had so long existed between them and their families had been cemented, by Bowline's never-to-be-forgotten services, into a love which forbade the idea of separation.

Oh, it was a pleasant sight to see that family circle in the evening time.   Around the whist table gathered the four elderlies —Captains E. and B. and their ladies, as intently occupied on the game as if fortunes were at stake.

The fair Bella, whom we described in the earlier portion of our history was not there, but Fred, not little " Fred" now, for he was a tall and elegant-looking young man, sat beside a beautiful girl, who from her resemblance to the Mrs. Edmiston described in our first chapter, would be recognized as Lettie, the daughter.   Bella had married, and found with a good and noble husband another home than her father's house.   Never was a happier family circle formed than that at which we may now cast a hasty glance.

A change has come over all its members since we have seen them, yet it is a calm and peaceful change ; such a change with the elder ones as comes upon the earth when summer gives place to a fair and glorious autumn ; such a change to the younger, as from bud-bearing spring into full-blossoming summer.

At the moment which we take to again introduce the reader to these, their old acquaintances, Captain Bowline was in great glee, for himself and Mrs. Edmiston had just won the second game of whist.

" That's the way me and your young wife go to windward

you, of Captain Edmiston !" said he—" her and me was born to luck."

" Not always to good luck on my part !" said she, sadly, and she sighed as she spoke. Perchance a thought of her lost child swept across her mind.

" Wall, I don't know, but I've an idee that you are one of them sort that's born to good luck, but it takes time for it to come. You know that just when you was in your worst fix, aboard my old craft, I found ye out—and I've known them sort o' people that always had good fortune come to them just when everything seemed darkest ahead."

" I wish that I could think so," replied the lady, " for then I might yet hope to see my son, my lost Edward."

" Wall, now I wouldn't wonder to see that youngster pop in here some time, jist when we don't expect—"

At this moment a heavy ring at the door bell was heard, and the old Captain, as he heard it, said—" Go to the door, Fred, and see who's there !"

Mrs. E.'s face paled as she heard the ring, for the words of Bowline had made a strange effect upon her, and she almost expected to see the image of her long-lost and darling child rise up before her. But the next moment, Frederick returned into the room with one whom, though years have also somewhat changed him, we can recognise as Captain Darlington.

" Why, Frank, God bless you, my friend ! I didn't expect you for over a month to come," said Edmiston, warmly, as he grasped the extended hand of the new comer.

" Well, sir, the Mary has given you a pleasant disappointment ! I believe she's the fastest ship in the trade. She's almost run away from us this trip ! I've only been seventy-three days out !"

" Wall, that beats the Turks !" exclaimed Bowline; " I'd like to take a trip in that ere craft of yours, Captain Darlington. I thought I'd sailed *some*, but this takes a double reef in everything that I've hearn tell of."

" It *is* a quick run," responded the new comer, " but I was confoundedly hurried when I was off the north-end of Madagascar, and maybe that helped me along some !"

" How so ?" asked Edmiston.

" Why, I was chased by about the fastest brig that ever cut salt water in two, and if she hadn't carried away her topmasts in pressing on canvass after me, I've an idea that you'd own one ship the less, and I'd have my berth-ticket in another world !"

" Why, was she a pirate ?"

" Yes, and none other than the one that has half broke up the English trade; a saucy devil that calls himself the King of the Sea, and makes a wide sweep in those waters !"

" How near did he get to you ?"

" Within the range of his guns ! I've got one of his thirty-two pound shot in the hull for a keep-sake !"

·" You must arm yourself for the next trip !"

" Arms wouldn't save us if we should fall in with him ! He's a regular dare-devil, and is well manned and armed. He beat off an English frigate in a running fight a few weeks before I sailed, and now they have a whole fleet upon the look-out for him. It is commanded by that devil Hawkhurst, who is now an Admiral, and I almost feel like taking sides with the pirate when I remember him and his rascally conduct."

" Of what nation is this pirate ?" asked Edmiston.

" I don't know of what nation the chief is---but he handles his craft, a regular clipper, as if he had been used to it ! "There is said to be a large gang of them, and I suppose they are a mixture of all nations. The Captain is represented to be a rather old fellow, with a long, black beard, and gray hair ! I was too busy in working the ship when they were in chase, to even raise a glass to look at her."

Young Frederick had been listening with deep attention to the remarks of Darlington, and now eagerly said :

" I wish I had been aboard with you, Captain Darlington ! I would so like to see a pirate !"

" So much the bigger fool, you," said his father; "the wider berth you give them the better would it be for you !"

" Is this one reported to be cruel and blood-thirsty ?" asked Lettie, timidly.

" Not always, lady, though it is feared that in some cases he has not only sunk the ships which he has captured, but destroyed the crews."

" Oh horrible; how can men, those who bear the image of their Maker, deface and destroy their own likeness !" said she, with deep feeling.

" Don't think of such things, dear Lettie," said her father; "go to your piano, and sing us a song which will chase away sad thoughts."

The fair girl obeyed, and seating herself before the instrument, played a few lively airs with exquisite taste and judgment. While she thus wiled away the sadness of the passing moment, the elder ones resumed their game of whist, and soon forgot the music and all things else save their immediate play.

CHAPTER XVIII.

The danger is near,
Yet little they fear
Who skim o'er the sea
So fearless and free.

THE pirate brig when she sailed from the harbour, as we described in our sixteenth chapter, stretched boldly out from the shore, heading up the channel directly in the track of the East Indiaman. The breeze was light, and every stitch of canvass which was bent to a spar was set to catch it. It was the commander's wish to got her out of the latitude of the rendezvous as soon as possible, for knowing that the English men-of-war were on the look-out for him, he wished to prevent, above all things, a discovery of the lurking place of his band. In a few hours the land was hidden from his view, and then shortening sail, he proceeded more leisurely on his cruise, his look-out from aloft carefully sweeping the sea in search of a sail.

Not long in that frequented channel had they to wait for the sight of a sail. On the evening of the third day out, a sail had been seen from the mast-head just as the sun sunk down into the western waters, and as she appeared to be standing down toward the brig, the latter took in all sail so as not to be seen, and then awaited the stranger's approach. As the darkness came on, the strange sail was lost to view, but as her course when last seen would bring her close by the brig, the commander of the latter patiently awaited her approach, first clearing his vessel for action, and making all ready for an engagement if the vessel which approached should prove to be armed.

The breeze was very light, scarcely rippling the waters of the channel, which rolled in long regular swells, without a break or spot of foam upon them. The mid hour of night had passed and still no sign of the stranger appeared. Bertram began to think that she had seen him before the darkness came on, and altering her course had passed him. Several times, after in vain sweeping his vision through the darkness with the aid of a night glass, had he been on the point of making sail on the brig, and had at last raised his trumpet to his lips, when Bernardo Consuelo, his first lieutenant, silently laid his hand upon his arm, and pointed to a whitish appearance in the darkness close off their lee quarter, but said not a word.

"It is she!" whispered Bertram. "Be silent, but have the starboard battery all ready to fire if I bid them."

Slowly the white mass drew on, and then sail after sail could be distinguished. She was a full rigged ship, standing dead before the wind, everything set which could draw below and aloft, steering by her course for the Isle of Ceylon. Her crew had evidently not discovered the pirate, for there was no confusion on board; indeed, as the brig had no sail set, and her hull and spars were as black as the night itself, it was not strange that she had escaped discovery.

The strange ship had now ranged nearly abreast of the brig's beam, and Bertram had raised his trumpet to hail and order her to heave-to, when the Spaniard, Consuelo, his lieutenant, who had been closely examining her with a glass, answered hastily:

"Speak not! Holy Virgin! we are lost if she discovers us! It is not a merchantman; it is a three-decker, and we are under the very muzzles of her guns."

It was well that the Spaniard made this timely discovery, for there was so little wind that the brig could not have escaped from under a fire so heavy as could have been poured into her by the man-of-war. Scarcely did the crew of the pirate breathe while the vast ship slowly passed on her course, and disappeared in the darkness. It now lacked but a few hours of daylight, and Bertram was anxious to haul off from so dangerous an antagonist. Therefore, as soon as the ship had passed entirely from sight, he sent a few hands aloft, directing them noiselessly to loose the brig's courses and topsails, which were as quietly sheeted home, and then as the brig gathered steerage-way, she was brought to the wind with yards sharp braced, so as to head in a direction nearly opposite to that of the ship.

Scarcely had she come up to the wind when another sail was discovered, standing in the same direction as the first; but this, from the trim of her yards and the set of her sails, was anything but a man-of-war. As she neared the brig, Bertram at once saw that she was an English East Indiaman, and for a moment the thought of her capture rested in his mind, but the close vicinity of her convoy and the lightness of the breeze, made the danger too apparent even for his reckless mind to pass over, and when the ship passing close to the windward of him, hailed, "Brig ahoy! Where are you from, and where bound to?"

He answered, "The brig Lucy Bertram, from Madras, bound home," and as he made no hostile demonstration, was not suspected as being other than a peaceable merchantman, for the night was yet too dark to note particulars.

Within a half hour after passing the second sail, two more were discovered, and now the pirates knew that they were in company with an outward-bound fleet of Indiamen, which of course were under convoy of a strong naval force.

Notwithstanding the lightness of the wind, which would render his escape difficult, Bertram determined to overhaul some of the merchantmen, which he knew were in the habit of taking out a great deal of specie, and to endeavour to relieve them of some of their valuables. Therefore, when the first dawn of light showed him a heavy merchantman, but a half mile to leeward of him, he squared away for her, and before her sleepy crew knew that a stranger was in the fleet, he lay alongside of her, grappled, and boarded her with only twenty or thirty of his men, capturing her without a single blow being made in resistance.

Great was the astonishment of the Captain when, surprised in his berth, he was awakened in his sleep to find his vessel in possession of the pirates, and the amount of the money he had on board demanded of him.

"By whose authority do ye this outrage?" cried he, almost maddened at the thought of being robbed in the very centre of the fleet.

"By the authority of our king!" answered a pirate, who again demanded the specie, with the ticklish point of a cutlass playing uncomfortably near his throat. "The King of the Sea requires tribute, and you had better bear a hand in its payment, else we've a way of hurrying ye?"

"Oh, God! how can I account to my owners for this surprise?" murmured the miserable man; "I am lost—ruined!"

"That's your look out, not ours!" shouted the pirate, harshly; and then, softening his tone as he saw Bertram descend into the cabin, he added: "Come, sir, hand over your specie, and let us be off about our business; we have other calls to make this morning."

"How can I ever account for this?" again murmured the unfortunate Captain, as he rose from his berth and permitted the keys, which hung above his head, to be taken down, and applied to a huge oaken chest which stood beside his berth.

"What amount have you on board, sir?" asked Bertram, sternly.

"Forty thousand pounds in golden sovereigns." was the answer.

"Hand me pen and paper!" again said Bertram. It was done, and after writing a hasty line, he said: "Bear that to your owners, or to the Admiral of the fleet, or to whom else it may concern. It is a receipt for the money which I have borrowed of them. Tell them, whenever they will call at the palace of Bertram, the King of the Sea, their money shall be returned with interest!" Then turning to his followers, he bade them bear the chest on board the brig, and, after spiking all the Englishman's guns, and binding the crew so that no signal could be made to the rest of the fleet, he cast off his grapnels, and, in a few minutes, was standing off upon a wind, with all sail set. He had not been observed by any of the fleet when he boarded the merchantman, as it was scarcely light; but when she was observed to be driving unmanaged before the wind, and he crowding all sail away from her, guns were fired, and signals made by the nearest merchantmen, which at once notified the men-of-war of his vicinity. These, with one exception, were already to leeward of him, and Bertram apprehended little difficulty in escaping; therefore, when he saw that he was discovered, he boldly hoisted his broad flag, and fired a shot to leeward as a signal of contempt and defiance. But too well was that flag known, and when the English vessels of war saw its broad folds displayed in the very midst of their fleet, immediate chase was made by them, while the merchantmen, as if still afraid of capture, crowded on their canvass in an opposite direction from that which would be crossed by the brig. There was but one English man-of-war to windward of the pirate, and she was in a position which did not much trouble Bertram, as he could take the wind abeam and still go to windward of the seventy-four and two frigates which were to leeward of him, having passed in the night. But the wind which had before been exceedingly light, now died entirely away, and all the vessels lay motionless.

The situation of the brig was now exceedingly perilous. The most distant of the men-of-war was not over six miles from her, while the nearest was almost within gun-shot. Bertram at once saw that if the calm lasted, a most overwhelming boat force could be brought against him, and already could the preparations be observed on board of the armed vessels. Silently his crew gazed up at the cloudless sky; calmly looked they upon the motionless water; quietly they gazed upon their enemies in the distance, and braced their hearts for the approaching trial. They were bold and desperate men, who in strife knew but two words, *victory* or *death !* Bertram bade his crew rig out their sweeps, but slow was the brig's progress with these. At last the boats of the English vessels, after communicating with each other, formed into three lines of attack and cautiously rowed down towards the brig, which could scarcely gather steerage way with her sweeps.

As he saw the fearful odds in numbers, for they seemed at least six or eight to one, the countenance of Bertram, which before had been calm and placid as the sky above him, lit up with a glow of wild excitement.

"Now, men, ye shall have such work as befits brave hearts and strong hands !" he shouted. "This is some relief to the paltry thieving of our profession. Double shot with canister those guns! Loosen your blades in their scabbards; look to your weapons, for this will be no child's play."

His orders were silently and quietly obeyed, for men bent on desperate resolves like these, waste not their breath in useless shouts or vain words.

From almost every ship in the fleet boats had been despatched, and now led by the heavy launches of the men-of-war, they rowed swiftly down upon the brig, cheering each other as they dashed on. They were formed in three lines, one heading for the stern, another for the beam, and the third for the bow of the brig.

"'Train the guns for the two forward boats !" shouted Bertram, and then as they approached within musket shot he waved his sword to the gunners who stood with the burning matches in their

hands. The signal was obeyed, and with a shock which shook the
brig from her keel upward, both of the heavily-loaded guns were
discharged upon the advancing foe.

Fearful was the effect of the grape and canister as it rained in
amongst them; the two leading boats were shattered and sunk, but
the remainder, amid shouts, curses and groans, dashed on. There
was no time for the pirates to reload their guns; the next moment
hundreds of the enemy were alongside, and the combat was
continued with pistol, pike, and cutlass. Awful was the carnage!
Twice had the English mounted the bulwarks of the brig, and each
time had they been driven back to their boats with fearful loss.
But a fresh arrival of boats from the fleet seemed about to decide

the fate of the day. Many of the pirate crew had fallen, many
more were wounded, and all were worn down with the strife against
such tremendous odds. Bertram's voice was heard above all the
dreadful din as he cheered his men on to exertion. Wherever the
foes were thickest, there gleamed his bloody sabre, and, as grass
before the scythe of the mower, they melted away before its terrible
sweep. He seemed a fated being, one whom shot nor steel could
harm. But even he grew faint and tired with slaying; one by one
his crew were dropping around him, and still fresh foes were
thronging in upon him. All seemed lost, yet he did not waver or
fall back, nor did one of his fearless crew. With them it was
indeed victory or death. They asked not for quarter—they gave

(11)

none! When he stood almost alone, parrying the blows of the foes who had gained the deck and almost surrounded him, Bertram felt the warm air which was almost stifling suddenly become cooler, and as he glanced upward at the sails he saw them fill with a rising breeze.

"On! On, men, one more effort and the day is ours! The breeze! the breeze!" shouted he, as again with rash fury he dashed forward upon the foe. "Consuelo—to the helm!" again he shouted, as the fresh breeze filled the flapping sails, and as the lieutenant, supported by a few of the crew, trimmed the braces and seized the helm, the brig gathered headway, and one by one the English boats were cut loose and left behind by the vessel. But a few brave and desperate men from the former had gained a footing, and now that their boats were gone and escape was impossible, they fought as despairing men only can fight. Bertram had been twice severely wounded by their leader, but now the sword of the latter was broken and he stood with folded arms awaiting his death, disdaining to ask for quarter where none could be expected. Already had a dozen swords been raised by the pirate band, who were maddened by their fearful loss, against the life of the gallant but defenceless foe—but Bertram beat down their murderous blades.

"Hold, strike him not! he is unarmed!" shouted he, and then for the first time his crew showed a mutinous spirit and cried—

"Slay all! Spare not an English dog! Look at our own dead! Revenge! Blood for blood!"

"Slaves! dare ye to thwart my will?" shouted their young leader —"Raise but one hand, speak ye but one more mutinous word and I'll show ye that I *am* your king!"

Then as his crew fell back abashed, he turned to the few of the English who survived, and added: "Throw down your weapons, and your lives shall be safe."

"I have none to throw down; if I had, I should not thus stand idly here, Sir Pirate!" said the English leader, sullenly.

"Sir, I respect your bravery, and it shall meet that reward at my hands which bravery and honour merit at the hands of the brave. Surrender, and on my honour, ye shall go free and uninured as soon as I can land ye."

"We have no other choice, but had his sword been as strong as his will, ye would not thus easily have captured Blount Hazlewood," said the English officer.

"No—judging from experience I think not," said Bertram, with a smile so different from his late fierce look of anger, that he did not seem to be the same being; and then as he cast his eye to his garments dripping with his own blood, he added, "I have a specimen of your skill and courage upon my own body which will not soon be forgotten; I believe I am severely wounded."

"The hand that has hurt you willingly will now as willingly aid you. I am a surgeon, and better skilled in the use of my instruments than the sword," now said the officer, whom the reader will recognise as an old friend, and whose sullen anger was much softened by the changed demeanor of his captor.

"I thank ye," replied Bertram; "as our own surgeon is amongst the killed, we will have great need of your assistance. I feel very faint. Consuelo, the brig will be safe now; bear away for our anchorage; we have had fighting enough for one cruise."

"Ay, one half of our men are dead, nearly all the rest are wounded."

"Poor fellows, their wives and children will feel this blow!" said the chief, sadly; and then as he glanced toward the English men-of-war, which were already in chase, he remarked to the surgeon: "Your vessels will have to be fleet, sir, to overtake this craft; if this breeze holds we will soon be well out of their reach."

"My God! where have I seen you before?" said the surgeon' who now for the first time regarded him attentively.

"Never have you seen me before, unless you before this have met our band. I have been with them from childhood, and now I am their chief."

"The King of the Sea? The daring freebooter of the Mozambique—and so young?"

"I am young, and yet these lawless men acknowledge no other king."

"I know not where, yet I must have met you before," said the surgeon; "but you look faint—your wounds must be stanched."

As the kind surgeon tore open the dress of the young chief to examine his wounds, his eye caught a glimpse of the miniature which Champ had given Bertram, and which the latter had worn around his neck. He raised it in his hand, and regarding it a moment with strange attention, exclaimed, "Good God! how strange is this! Know ye whose is this likeness?"

"No—I do not, with certainty," said Bertram, faintly; "but why do you ask? why this surprise? Have you ever seen it before?"

"I have seen him from whom it was painted, as sure as there is truth in me!"

"Oh, was he—is he my father?" gasped the wounded chief, who, ere an answer could be given, fainted from loss of blood, and was borne below. Meanwhile the vessel sped swiftly homeward before a freshening breeze, followed still by the English ships of war, which, however, were gradually losing ground. It was in the morning, three days after the battle with the boats, that the brig worked into the old anchorage in the bay which fronted the village of the Sea-king. Bertram, faint and feeble, was upon her deck, but not able to move about or give the necessary orders for working the vessel, which duty was performed by Consuelo, his lieutenant. Bertram was supported by the kind English surgeon, who uttered many expressions of surprise as the brig, rounding the point of the island which guarded the harbour, brought him within view of the beautiful village; and when he saw women and children crowding down upon the green shores of the bay, shouting their cheers of welcome to the loved ones who had returned, his surprise was but increased.

"Poor things! unto sad disappointment are many of them doomed!" said Bertram, mournfully, as his eye fell upon the gleeful groups who were there gathered along the shore.

"What ship is that?" asked the surgeon, pointing to a tall and stately vessel which lay at anchor close in shore, and from which several boats were carrying packages and bales of merchandise to the land.

"A prize, I presume by her looks!" answered Bertram. "Some of our band have been more successful than I in the last cruise."

The brig had now reached her anchorage, and amid the cheers of their comrades on shore and aboard the other vessels, she rounded to, dropped her anchor, and in a few moments lay as quiet with her sails snugly furled, as if she had never seen battle or storm.

The wounded chief was carefully borne to his home on shore, whither he was accompanied by the surgeon, who in their short acquaintance had become strangely attached to him, and seemed deeply interested in his recovery.

CHAPTER XIX.

The strangest chapter in our history
Where light breaks forth on mystery;
Where warm tears are wildly flowing,
And sweet smiles are brightly glowing;
Where deadly foes have met to die,
Where loudest rings the battle cry.

It was not until the second day after he had been landed that Bertram was able to receive the reports of the officers regarding the capture of the merchant ship which he had seen at anchor on coming into port with the brig.

The captains of the three proas who had been engaged in her capture stood by his bedside on this day; and that their prize had not been taken without a heavy resistance, one might judge from the appearance of these officers, who all bore the marks of recent wounds which were yet freshly bandaged.

"Where made ye your prize, and when?" asked the chief.

"On the first day of our cruise, but a few leagues to leeward of the Comoras!"

"Did ye lose many men?"

" Near one third of our crews ; the ship was stoutly manned and armed, and her crew fought long and well."

" Were many of them slain ?"

" But few. They fought behind their high bulwarks, and were sheltered until we boarded them, when our numbers overpowered them. The Captain is badly wounded, as also a brave and most desperate passenger, who had a wife and daughter on board."

" Where are they ?"

" Confined as prisoners, awaiting your orders regarding their disposal !"

" It is well—let them be kindly cared for ; you know my laws regarding captives !"

" We do, and have in this case obeyed them, though it was hard to restrain our crews from revenging their fallen comrades."

" They must learn obedience, mercy, and forbearance. You say that the Captain of the prize is dangerously wounded ?"

" He is ; our surgeon thinks that he will not live."

" May I not visit him ? Perhaps I can be of assistance to the poor fellow !" said Hazlewood.

" Certainly !" answered Bertram. " You are as free as any of my band to go or come, or do what ye will, and you cannot ask that which I will not grant."

" Thank ye—thank ye ! I'd like to see those poor wounded prisoners, for I might be of some use to them—I've had a deal of practice in gun-shot wounds and cuts !"

" These gentlemen will conduct you to their prisoners, and obey any directions you may give concerning them. Harkye, gentlemen ; this Dr. Hazlewood is my friend—treat him as such !" responded the chief.

The officers bowed obedience, and retired with Hazlewood. In a few moments afterward the latter was ushered into the room where the wounded Captain of the prize lay.

Pale, motionless, and almost pulseless, lay the unfortunate man. A broad gash had seamed his high and noble forehead, bandages were passed around various parts of his body, betokening the fearful injuries he had received. His matted hair hung down over his pallid brow, his dim eye wandered restlessly to and fro in the room as if it sought for the face of a single friend among so many enemies.

" Poor fellow !" said Hazlewood, as he took the sufferer's hand within his own and felt the low feverish pulse.

The sound of pity must have been something new to the invalid, for his eyes brightened with interest, and he moved his lips as if trying to speak, when the sound of the kind doctor's voice fell upon his ear. But the latter noted not the glance of the invalid's eye, nor heeded he his attempt to speak—his own eye was riveted on a ring which encircled a finger of the hand which he had raised. It was a large red cornelian, and the graving on it was such as once seen would not easily be forgotten.

Hazlewood gave one more long steady look at the massive seal ring, then bent earnestly over the face of the sufferer, as if he would read his fate in his features.

"Good God, how altered!" said he: "yet it must be him! This ring—he never would have parted with it—it must be he! Darlington! Darlington! Oh, my friend, is this you?"

The helpless invalid could not speak, but a look of consciousness beamed from his eyes, for he had heard his name called, and that in kindly tones. The look was recognised, and Hazlewood knelt and wept beside his friend, whom for years he had not met. But soon he recovered his calmness, and at once exerted his skill in examining and attending to the wounds of the unfortunate sufferer, who was indeed in a most critical situation.

After attending to this case, and administering a pleasant opiate to relieve the present pain of the sufferer, he demanded to be conducted to the room of the passenger, whom the Captains had represented as having fought so bravely, and whom he was informed was also wounded.

What was his surprise to recognise in him another friend, and that friend no other than Captain Edmiston, who was but slightly wounded, and whom he found sitting in company with two ladies, whom, from their dress and appearance, he correctly conjectured to be the wife and daughter of whom he had heard the pirate captain speak.

Oh, how glad was the meeting of these friends, the more so that it was the least expected.

"How is this?" exclaimed Edmiston, as he warmly met the greeting of the noble-hearted surgeon. "Do I find Doctor Hazlewood amongst pirates?"

"Ay, but not one of them. I, like yourself, am a prisoner, but am kindly treated."

"For Heaven's sake, explain! Into what kind of hands have have we fallen? These poor females—"

"Are as safe as if they were at their own homes, if I judge aright of the strange being who leads this band, and who with them holds the title of the King of the Sea, and a kingly way he has with him, too."

"I have heard of him before; my ship has been chased by him."

"Your ship? I was told that you were a passenger on board of the vessel which they captured."

"I was, but also was the owner of the ship. I had taken passage for the trip only, for the benefit of my daughter's health."

"Is she sick?" and as the doctor spoke, he glanced kindly toward the fair girl, whose eyes met his with a look so like one that he had lately seen, that he involuntarily started to his feet. "Have you another child, Captain Edmiston?" asked he, hurriedly, as he still gazed upon the face of the daughter.

"I had one, but I expect he is not in this world; he was torn from his mother's side in infancy."

"Great Heaven! It must be! How strange and mysterious are the ways of Providence!" exclaimed the Doctor, as he rushed from the room, leaving Edmiston and his family in a strange state of surprise, utterly unable to account for his singular conduct.

When Hazlewood left the Edmiston family, he hastened to the bedside of Bertram. "The miniature! Let me see the miniature!" cried he, almost out of breath with haste and agitation. The young chief permitted him to examine it. "It must be he! It is? Know you aught regarding your early history?" asked he of Bertram, with increased agitation.

"Nothing, but that I was torn from my home and my parents while yet an infant, adopted by the chief of this band, and have been reared as a pirate."

"How came you by this miniature?"

"All is explained in the diary which lays on yonder table. The miniature was clasped around my neck by this same braid of dark hair, when I was stolen by the pirates—or so their chief has told me. I have ever fancied that it was the likeness of my father."

"It is, and he is—"

"Where? Oh, do you know him? Have I a living father?"

"Be calm—be quiet! Be calm as I am, and I'll—I'll tell you all!" said the doctor, who was anything but calm himself.

"Well, well, relieve my anxiety. There must be something in this, or you would not act so strangely."

"Your father is—no, I don't know that *he* is your father. Let me take that miniature and diary with me for a short time. I will return soon."

"Take them; but do explain this strange mystery of words and actions."

"I will in a few moments, when I return!" exclaimed the doctor, as he left the room with the miniature and the pirate's diary.

In a few moments the Edmiston family saw him entering the room, his face radiant with pleasure and excitement.

"I have found—"

"What?" asked Edmiston, almost inclined to think that the doctor had lost his senses.

"Have you ever seen this miniature?" said he, holding it up to their view.

"By Heaven, it is my own! Where got you it?" exclaimed Edmiston, with wonder.

But Mrs. Edmiston, when her gaze fell upon it, spoke not. Her face turned pale; she stepped nearer to it—her eyes fell upon some blood which stained it—she remembered where she had last seen it —where she had last placed it; and, then her form quivered and reeled—"Lost, lost!" she shrieked, and fell senseless to the floor.

"Oh, my poor wife! Why is this, doctor; for the love of Heaven explain!" cried Edmiston, as he bent over the fallen form of her who had fainted.

" I will directly, when she comes to. Don't weep, young lady," said he, turning to Lettie ; " it is only a fainting fit, and you shall have more cause to laugh than to weep. I have joyful news in store for you."

" My son—pirates—dead, dead !" murmured the poor mother, as she slowly recovered, and partly unclosed her eyes.

" No, no, madam ! not dead—cheer up !"

" Not dead ? Oh, God, the miniature ! On the dreadful night, when I lost him for ever, to please his childish fancy, I hung that miniature about his neck ; and now for the first time I see it since then—and look—!" she screamed, as she snatched it from the hand of the doctor ; " there's blood, red blood upon it. Oh, God, my child, my poor child ! Lost, lost !"

" No, no, he still lives !" cried the doctor, as the big tears rolled down his cheeks, for a heart of stone would have melted in the presence of that mother's grief.

" Doctor, dare not deceive my poor wife ; raise not false hopes to break her heart with !"

" Sir, I do not deceive you ! If you and your lady will only be calm, as I am—be calm, I will explain all to you, and prove that your son not only lives but is even now near you."

" Where, oh, where ?" cried the mother, looking as if she would have leaped through walls of stone or grated bars to meet her boy —the idol of her memories.

" Be calm, sit down, and let us investigate the proofs," said the doctor, trembling in every nerve as he opened the diary which Bertram had given him to examine. " Here's a book, written in a confounded bad hand, the diary of Robert Champ. Let's see, it was commenced in Boston, year 1825, and runs through his career as a pirate. Whew! wouldn't this be a prize for some poor devil of a novel writer !"

" What has that book to do with your promised explanation ?" cried Edmiston, anxiously waiting some relief to his suspense.

" A good deal, if I can only find the place ; but be cal m—be calm as I am. When was your son lost ?" said the doctor, still hurriedly running over the blotted leaves of the book.

" In the summer of 1825," answered the Captain.

" Eighteen hundred and twenty five, ah, yes ; let me see, August—"

" It was the first evening in August ; never, never, shall I forget it !" exclaimed Mrs. Edmiston now a little more composed.

" Well ;" continued the Doctor, " let me see, here's July, August, yes, August first, it reads ; had a rich haul to-night, abducted a lady, got one thousand dollars for it, and a baby thrown in; carried her on board a ship in the bay: named the boy Bertram, and adopted him as my own. Believe he's the son of an English lord, or else in the way of one. The work was done for Lord Clarence.' "

"Oh, God, this certainly means my boy!" cried the mother, "for that villain Clare went by that name."

"What is all this? For heaven's sake let me understand it!" exclaimed Edmiston, almost mad with impatience.

"It is simply this. I know who and where your son is. This book from which I have been reading, is the private log-book of one Robert Champ, who was lately the chief of this gang of pirates. By this book you see that he has had something do with the loss of your boy. If you'll be calm a moment, and let your lady explain how he was taken, we can easily get at the truth of the matter!"

Hurriedly, but plainly, did Mrs. Edmiston now relate to the Doctor the occurrences which the reader is already acquainted with. As she finished, the Doctor exclaimed:—

"I see through it all now, and your boy is —"

"Where, oh, where?"

"On this very spot, or at least within a hundred yards. He is the King of the Sea, the chief of these pirates."

"Oh, God, it were better if we had never found him, than to have thus discovered him in crime and infamy!" groaned the father.

"I'm not so sure of that!" replied the Doctor warmly: "he has been reared by bad hands to a bad profession, but he has a noble heart and honourable mind, and it is not too late to save him."

"Oh, let me see him, he cannot be a pirate! Oh, he will not be one when he sees a kneeling mother before him. Oh, let me see him, my long-lost, ever-loved son!" cried the weeping mother.

"I must prepare him for the meeting; the shock must not come too suddenly upon him, for he is weak, and ill!" said the Doctor, and he hurried from the room, to execute this delicate but pleasant duty.

How he succeeded the reader may imagine when we inform him that a few hours afterwards the chamber of Bertram contained his parents and his sister, all of whom were kneeling in prayer by his bed-side, offering up their gratitude to the kind Providence which, in its own mysterious way, had reunited them.

When they had arisen from their bended knees, and while the full-hearted mother pressed her warm lips to her son's pale brow, the good Doctor who had gone to visit Captain Darlington, returned to the room.

As he entered it, and saw the smile of happiness which rested on each face there, he burst into tears. It seemed the only way in which his heart, so full of joy, could relieve itself. It was a strange compound which formed his nature. Brave as a lion, yet tender as a woman.

"How is Darlington?" asked Edmiston, as the Doctor became more calm.

"Better; decidedly better. He'll live now. He shan't die when everything is coming out so bright and clear."

(12)

"I hope not!" said Bertram. "I hope that I shall **never** have another death to account for at the hands of my band."

"I thank Almighty God for those words!" said the mother. "Now, indeed, you are my own Edward. You are not a *pirate now.*"

"Alas, my mother, will the world say so?"

"The world, my son! The world shall not have you. You are mine, mine for ever."

"You will not follow your present fearful calling, will you, my brother?" asked poor Lettie, while the tears of joy streamed down her pale cheeks.

"No, my sister. I have found parents and a sister. My band have lost their King, if they will not with me give up their present life."

"Hark! what does the sound of those guns mean?" asked the Doctor, as the reports of several cannon in the distance were plainly heard.

Before an answer could be given, Consuelo, the Spanish lieutenant next in command to Bertram, rushed into the room.

"Our retreat is discovered. The English are upon us!" exclaimed he, hurriedly. "Their force is advancing into the harbour."

"Are they in boats; or have they found the channel with their vessels?"

"In boats; but their force is heavy. They have paused on the island, either to arrange some plan of attack, or to wait for reinforcements."

"Warp the brig alongside the shore, and lay her batteries broadside on to them. Muster all hands to their weapons! I am weak, but I will not desert them now."

"Oh, my son, peril not your life now. Let me not lose you the moment that you are found."

"Mother, I am yet the chief of this band. Though they are pirates, I must not desert them. I must drive back this force, or all will perish. This shall be my last battle!"

A short time afterwards, Bertram stood upon the beach with his drawn sabre in his hand. Pale and feeble seemed he, but his eye again flashed with the wild excitement of approaching battle. As he stepped forth among his men, loud rose their shout—

"Long live Bertram the brave! Long live the King of the Sea! Death to all our foes!" and, as if it joined in their feeling, the strange flag of their King flapped gaily out upon the breeze, while the stern figure which was embroidered upon its rich folds seemed almost to be a living being.

Edmiston and Hazlewood had accompanied Bertram to the water-side, and now the surgeon was intently gazing upon the movements of the party, who had paused upon the banks of the island about half a mile distant, apparently preparing for the attack.

"I think you will recognise that tall man in uniform, who is apparently in command of the English forces!" said Hazlewood to Edmiston, handing him the spy-glass which he had been using.

" I cannot, he is too distant for me to note his features!" replied the latter, after looking toward the enemy.

" You have not seen him so lately as I have," responded the Doctor; " it is Lord Hawkhurst."

" What! my old and fiendish enemy! Edward, give me, too, a weapon! I stand not here idle, when he who has caused all our troubles is before me. The leader of yonder party is he who has led you to this life, who has been my fiendish persecutor."

"He shall meet his punishment, but they are about to advance. I pray you to retire, my father. I shall easily beat them off."

" Their numbers are far greater than yours, and they are English seamen, by English officers led; they will fight well!" responded Edmiston.

" But with them it is not victory or death, as with us. They can retreat; we cannot. Better had they attacked a caravan of hungry lions than meet men like mine, with their wives and children at their backs, and no alternative but victory or the pirate's death of shame "

" I join in the defence; give me a weapon!" was the father's calm reply; and again the pirates shouted as they saw the passenger whom, to their sorrow, they had before time found so brave, join to meet the foe.

" I can't fight my own countrymen!" said Hazlewood, "but I can be of use to the wounded; I shall be near you: but see, they are advancing."

The English force was indeed upon the advance. The boats were scattered apart so as to make as little mark for the pirate's guns as possible, and they were many in number.

The arrangement for defence on the part of the pirates was very excellent.

The brig and smaller vessels were laid in alongside of the beach with their broadsides bearing directly upon the approaching boats. The crews of all were at their quarters, and even many of the boldest of the women and the largest of the boys had gathered down upon the shore with weapons in their hands.

The chief of the pirates stepped on board of his vessel, and, as he passed along her decks, he spoke low words of encouragement to the crew, who now in silence trained their guns upon the advancing enemy. Standing each at his post, they gazed upon the approaching boats with that calm resolve to do or die which always equalises numbers, let the odds be ever so great.

" Reserve your fire to the last moment; and when you hear the order, lose not a shot!" said Bertram in a low calm tone, which, however, was heard by every one on board, so deep and full was his voice. The boats of the English were now almost within musket-shot. Their commander could be distinguished by his uniform and the rash bravery which induced him to stand in the very bows of the leading boat.

As they came so near that the dash of their oars could be plainly heard, the pirate chief raised a silver speaking-trumpet to his lips.

"For the love of your own lives, hold back!" he shouted. "Ye come but to die."

"Surrender! Down with your colours and arms!" and then with a loud, wild cheer his boats dashed even more swiftly on. But ere the echo of that shout had died away, one word had been spoken by the pirate chief.

"*Fire!*" and ere another instant the thunder of the artillery, the hail of iron, the crash of splintered boats and oars, the shrieks of the wounded and dying, the gurgling cries of the drowning, mingled with the answering shout of defiance from the lips of the pirates. Dark and thick was the smoke cloud that for a moment veiled the boats from sight, but in a moment dark forms were seen in its thickness, and all of the boats which had not been sunk by that first dreadful fire, were alongside, and still their crews more than doubled the number of the pirates.

Deadly, wild, and hellish was now the strife. Hand to hand, and breast to breast, shouting, yelling and cursing, fought the foes. Hawkhurst had escaped the fire and was the first to spring upon the brig's deck. He knew the chief by his voice of command, and with a bound of eagerness, sprang to meet him. Nor did the other falter in the meeting. He remembered his father's words before the battle, and his hand met his heart's desire for revenge. He knew not half the villany of the man before him, yet he knew that damning wrong had been done. They met, and for an instant their swift blades, as they struck, lunged, and parried, could scarcely be seen. But soon the blows of Bertram became more and more weak. His strength was failing him, and his crew were all too busily engaged to see his situation or to aid him. But one eye had been upon him since the commencement of the combat. It was his father, but he was now separated from him by a circle of foes whom he in vain attempted to break through, but when he saw Bertram's sword fly from his hand, with one mad bound, though wounded on all sides, he dashed into the opposing ranks, but still could not reach the spot.

"Hold! Hawkhurst, spare my son!" he shouted, as he saw the sword of his enemy raised above the head of the defenceless chief.

Hawkhurst heard the cry of Edmiston! One glance at the face of the father, another at the son, and he seemed to divine the truth. A gleam of hellish joy sparkled in his eye, he raised the weapon which for a moment he had stayed, and shouted,

"Now is the hour of my revenge! He is your son? Then see him die!"

But the moment's delay sufficed to save the fallen youth, for what could not a father's strength do in such a moment! With one sweeping, crushing blow, Edmiston clove down the last foe who had stood between him and Hawkhurst, and with his own blade parried the blow which was aimed at the heart of his son. Then before the other could regain his ground, he drove his sabre up to the very hilt in his bosom.

"O, curse ye! At last your triumph is complete!" groaned Hawkhurst, as he fell to the deck. He spoke no more; his heart's last life-drop was shed. With the fall of their leader the English grew dispirited, more feeble were their efforts, and after a brief struggle the survivors retreated to their boats and pushed from the vessels.

But twice ere they reached the island from which they had last embarked, did the pirates pour in the fearful broadsides of their cannon upon them, and each time with fearful effect. But a few reached the shore in safety, and when they saw that the pirates were about to launch their boats in pursuit, they hoisted the white flag for mercy.

Scornful was the shout of the enraged and triumphant pirates, when they saw the white truce-flag fling its folds out upon the breeze.

"Blood for blood! Revenge for our fallen comrades!" was their mad cry, as they hastened to follow and complete the work of destruction.

But in this they were stayed by their chief.

"Stay!" he cried, "enough has been done this day. They shall be our prisoners! Consuelo, take ye a guard of obedient men, and receive the arms of the enemy, giving them their lives on their unconditional surrender! Dare not to murmur! It is my will!" added he, as he saw the sullen clouds of discontent gather upon their brows. Such was the force of discipline, that they dared not to disobey him.

One hour afterwards the remnant of the British forces were standing before the house of the King of the Sea, disarmed and sad in the uncertainty of their fate. They knew that they were in the hands of pirates, men of blood, with whom mercy was a thing unknown, pity a feeling to which they were strangers.

But two of their officers had survived the disgrace of defeat, and these were now confronted by the young chief, who though exceedingly weak from his recent exertions and former injuries, had passed through this battle unscathed.

"Of what force are ye?" asked Bertram. "Do ye belong to the regular fleet on the East India station?"

"No, we belong to an expedition which for months has been in chase of you, under Lord Hawkhurst, our Admiral, who is among the slain!" answered one, who appeared to be the highest in rank.

"Who now commands your vessels, and where are they?"

"I am the senior surviving officer, sir, but you must excuse me if I refuse to say where our vessels are. Nearly all their crews are destroyed, but they would not be captured without a blow."

"I do not wish to capture them—but you and your men are at liberty to seek them on one condition. It is, that for one week you do not return to this spot, or move from the place where they are anchored at this time."

"We can make no refusal to anything you offer. We are in your power!" answered the English officer.

"Then pledge your honour to the conditions which I have named, and you are free!".

"I do—but you seem very unlike the blood-thirsty King of the Sea whom we have so long sought for. This mercy is unexpected."

"The brave deserve favour from the brave, sir. Go, and when you next come to attack the King of the Sea in his own place of rest, come better prepared. I dislike to be disturbed when I'm on shore, I would rather meet my foes where blue water may serve to save me the trouble of digging their graves."

The English officer was about to turn away, when a strange figure coming from the direction of the late battle-ground met his view, and he paused with an expression of surprise.

The person who arrested his attention was no other than the good Doctor Hazlewood, who, with his coat off, his sleeves rolled up, and his hands, in which he held several amputating instruments, dripping with the blood of the poor fellows whose wounds he had been attending to, now approached.

"Why, Captain Danvers, is that you? I'm glad to see you alive, after this the hardest fight I've ever seen."

"Doctor Hazlewood! Why, sir, I thought you had been killed. You were reported as slain, by your own vessel, which we spoke the day before we fitted out for this attack. How came you here?"

"By the same luck, that has just befallen you. I'm a prisoner; but as well treated as if I was amongst our own men."

"So it would seem, sir, by the manner in which you have employed yourself. It must require *some* gratitude for an officer of your integrity to be found administering aid and comfort to a gang of pirates," said the officer, sternly.

"I have but done my duty as a humane man, sir!" responded the doctor.

"And your noble conduct shall not be forgotten by the *gang of pirates* whom this officer seems to hold in such contempt, forgetful of two lessons which he has learned of them, and which should at least entitle them to respect under the shadow of their own banner."

"I beg your pardon, sir!" stammered the officer, abashed by the stern reproof; and then he added, "I spoke hastily, and with the *official* duty of Dr. Hazlewood in my mind, not his humanity."

"It is well, sir; your boats are free to depart when you wish, but remember the conditions!" answered the young chief.

"If Captain Danvers and his men are about to leave and I am

free, it will be my *official duty* to request to be permitted to return to my ship with him, Captain Bertram, or, as I may now call you, Captain Edmiston !" said the surgeon, as he noted that the English officer was about to take advantage of the permission to depart.

The latter, as he heard Hazlewood speak to the chieftain by the name of Edmiston, turned quickly upon him :

" Edmiston !   Who did you address by that name ?" asked he.

" Him who has just given you freedom !" was the response.

" Is he—the King of the Sea—is *he* named Edmiston ?   Is he from England ?"

" You have spoken his name—but not his birth-place.   He was born on the mad ocean !   Doth it not fit him well to be a king upon the sea ?   But why asked you of his name and birth-place ?" asked the person alluded to.

" Because I am related to a family of that name in England, and I know not why, but your face seems strangely familiar to me."

" More mystery, more developments !" said Hazlewood, as he listened with interest to the conversation.   And then, as he saw Captain Edmiston coming from the house where his wife and daughter had awaited, with fear and trembling, the issue of the battle, the surgeon added : " Here comes one, Captain Danvers, that can probably give you all information regarding name and family."

" Holy Heaven ! it is my own cousin, Samuel Edmiston, whom I see !" exclaimed the officer, as he hastened to meet the new-comer.

" Edgar Danvers !   Little did I expect to meet you here !" said Edmiston, as he grasped the outstretched hand of the Englishman.

" And as little did I dream of meeting you !" replied the other. " Why, I have thought you dead !   You had left England, and gone, no one knew whither, and now—how came you here ?"

" A prisoner ; but, in losing my liberty, I have found that which would make slavery a blessing."

" Explain, my cousin, I do not understand you."

" I have here found a long-lost, an only son."

" A son !   What mean you ?   What, or whom ?"

" Look at that brave boy, who stands there pale and weak from the toil of battle.   Look on him, who, with an inferior force, has conquered even *English* seamen."

" I see him, that strange being, who calls himself the King of the Sea."

" He is *my son !*"

" Your son ?   An Edmiston a pirate ?   No, no, you jest ; and yet he is so like !   Oh, God ! I hope this is not true, that he so young, so brave, just in reach of a noble heritage—alas, that he should be an outlaw !"

" A heritage !   What know you of his heritage ?"

" Have you not heard of the death of your only brother, who **succeeded Sir Lancelot to the title and estate ?**"

" Indeed, I have not."

" Before I left England his will was read. He died without a child, he having never married, and in his will left everything to his brother's son, if his brother had one; otherwise, no son being born unto his brother to take the title and property, it was to revert to the nearest male relative of our branch, and, in both cases, to be taken on condition that the heritor should reside upon the estate, and keep up the old baronial customs."

" It is a vast and magnificent heritage ! Alas, that my son should be an outlaw !"

" There is some strange mystery here, which I cannot comprehend ! He is *your* son, and yet a pirate. For Heaven's sake let me know; I may yet be of service in this matter !" exclaimed Danvers.

" If you will go apart with me for a brief space, I will explain all," replied the other; and, the first having willingly acceded, they retired to the building which Edmiston had just left.

As they left the spot, the young chief turned sadly to Hazlewood, who had stood, in silent amazement, listening to these new discoveries :—

" Doctor !" said he, " you are determined to leave me, it seems. It is hard to part with new-found friends when you have just learned to love and appreciate them."

" It is my *official* duty to return to the service which supports me ; but—"

" But what, my friend ?"

" Why, I'd rather amputate ten legs than leave you, and your noble father, and Darlington, and—" The doctor seemed much confused, and suddenly broke off without finishing his sentence.

" Why the pain will be mutual if you leave us ; but is it necessary ?"

" *Necessary !* I must return to my ship ! I have no heritage. I depend on my profession."

" But I have gold."

" But I cannot be a pirate !" was the brief, cold reply of the doctor.

" You need not be, you will not be, if you remain with me."

" How ? Are you not the King of the Sea ?"

" *To-day* I am, but to-morrow may—"

" Oh ! what of to-morrow ?" asked the other, eagerly.

" Hazlewood, you have heard from one whom my father knows, and who seems to be a truthful and honourable man (he is brave, and honour and truth go hand in hand with bravery), that I am the heritor of a noble title and a rich estate !"

" I have, and would to God that now you were safe upon it."

" Hear me further ; I am the only son of my father, and the last of my name."

" Yes, and a noble race it hath ever been."

"It shall yet uphold its name and honour—I will claim and hold my right."

"Oh! if that could be; but you are—"

"*Outlawed!* yes, speak the hateful word! *Outlawed*, because in my helpless childhood I was torn, by an act of villany, from the parents who would have reared me in virtue and honour, and have been reared up to crime, which I was taught to believe right and honourable."

"Ay—who could blame you? and yet the world and its laws will hear no palliation; but why need the world recognise you? But few know your secret, they will not divulge it. You can escape from here, and—"

"What!" interrupted the other, "should I steal away from my band and steal into the world, and there live in perpetual fear of discovery? No! No!—I will go from here openly. I will enter England openly! It takes me not long to think or plan; Hazlewood, my course is laid. I have now seventy or eighty Englishmen in my power, and three of them, including yourself, are valuable officers to her Majesty's service."

"What mean you! not to—"

"Wrong a single one of ye, but hear me. I shall yet keep ye as my prisoners."

"What! and retract the liberty you have just given us? Is this honour?"

"Wait and hear before you condemn! You shall all be my prisoners on parole."

"On parole! Are you losing your senses? There is no—"

"Hear my whole plan before you again interrupt me. It has been formed since I have stood upon this spot, yet every item will I carry out. You see my father's ship lying at anchor out in the bay. Within a week that ship sails for England, bearing Captain Danvers, his men and officers, you included; and my father, mother, and—"

"Will Miss Lettie go?" interrupted the doctor again, while a most singular blush lit up his blunt countenance.

"Why do you interrupt me? Yes, she and all; Darlington as well as the rest, all save my own band, will return in that ship, which will be commanded by—"

"Who? Darlington won't be fit for duty this six months!"

"She shall be commanded by the King of the Sea!"

"By you? Oh! go not to England to be hanged."

"I go not there to be hanged; the hemp will never grow that can raise me between heaven and earth for a gaping crowd to gaze upon. I go to England to exchange prisoners and conclude a treaty of peace."

"My friend, why do you jest on a subject like this?"

"I do not jest. I shall take all of them to England, and shall release them on their parole of honour to consider themselves my

(13)

prisoners till I am free and have succeeded in obtaining a pardon for all that has occurred."

" And your band ?"

" Shall be disbanded. To-morrow that flag, which has become but too well known, shall be furled for ever."

" Will they disband ?   Will they let you leave them ?"

" Have not other monarchs abdicated ?   They dare not thwart my will."

" I fear for you; yet if all things turn out as you wish, I shall, indeed, be happy !"

" Not happier than I, in the love of my parents and sister, and —but why do you sigh and look so grave all at once ?"

" I don't know, but, but—" The Doctor again stammered, blushed, and came to a full stop.

" But what ? There's something the matter with you."

" Yes, I'm sick."

" You look not pale, nor wear the semblance of one that is ill. What think you is the matter ?"

" It is something that I can't cure—I may as well speak, though I know how hopeles—Captain Bertram, or Edmiston, or—I know not what to call you—I'm in love !" Deeper than ever was now the poor Doctor's blush ; greater than ever his confusion.

" With whom ? I'm sure your case cannot be desperate. Such diseases generally work their own cure, I'm told."

" I love—I love—confound it ! I can't get her name up out of my heart into my lips. I love Miss Lettie. There, I've said it !" and as the Doctor spoke he heaved a deep sigh, and wiped the perspiration which had gathered on his brow.

" My sister ?"

" Yes, she's an angel ! I've loved her since the first hour we met."

" Well, my friend, you shall have all opportunities of knowing her, and you may find that your feelings are reciprocated. A long passage on ship-board will be a fine opportunity to get acquainted. You know my plans, I shall go to my mother to make her happy with a knowledge of them ; and by-the-way, while I am there, shall I—no, no, I'll let you tell her yourself."

" I hope I shall make a better job of it than I did in telling you," muttered the Doctor, as the young chief walked away. And, then, as he glanced at his apparel and hands, he added : " But she musn't see me in this fix. The sooner I'm in my quarters and changing my rig the better."

And off hurried the noble fellow, his heart considerably lightened by the disclosure he had just made.

CHAPTER XX.

Farewell to the flag which waved o'er me,
  The conquering shield of the brave ;
Farewell to the good craft which bore me
  Through calm and the tempest's wild wave ;
Farewell, my brave comrades, for ever ;
  Long, long have we roamed o'er the tide ;
We part, but our parting shall never
  The thread of remembrance divide.

It was a sweet bright morning. The sun had just risen, and, as it shone upon the leaves, and grass, and flowers, which bent with the large bright dew-drows as if they had been weeping for the loss of the previous day, all things seemed beautiful.

"This is a lovely spot!" said Captain Danvers to Captain Edmiston, as they stood upon the portico of the chief's house, which fronted on the green toward the bay.

"And yet we must leave it," said the young chief, who, with folded arms, was standing by them, watching the gathering groups of men, who were assembling around a flag-staff, a few yards in front of the house as he had ordered them. When they were all mustered, the young chief stepped forward to the edge of the portico, where his eye could command, and his voice be heard by, all. "I have sent for ye, men, to advise with ye in our present situation," said he. It is known to ye that our rendezvous being discovered, we are no longer safe from attack; and, that, though we have repelled one invasion, we never shall be at rest here, for numbers will weigh down courage and perseverance. You see the necessity of a change of quarters, of a new rendezvous!" A low murmur of assent arose from the crowd. "Where shall we go?" There was no answer. He continued: "Where can we now find a place to locate in safety? Where can ye place your wives and children where they may rest undisturbed?" Still no answer; but as each looked at the other, that entire band seemed to feel that they were indeed outlaws. "I have a plan for ye, will ye abide by my will?"

"Long live Bertram the brave! Where you lead, there will we follow!" was the answering shout.

A sad smile of pleasure lighted the countenance of the young chief at this exhibition of his control over their hearts and wills, and he continued.

"You have treasures and gold in store enough to make all of you independent for ever. It is all safe in the treasury magazine, of which I hold the key. Bernardo Consuelo! Robert Armstrong! Albert Carroll! Pierre Lausanne! my captains and my friends, come-hither!" The four persons named advanced from amongst their crews with whom they had been standing. The chief took from his belt a heavy key, and handing it to Consuelo, continued:

"I appoint ye, gentlemen, to distribute equally man to man, to each one of the band, the contents of that magazine of treasure—reserving no share for myself !"

" What means this ?" asked they, in surprise ; " by our compact, when the band was formed, this was only to occur when all agreed to separate for ever !"

" Ay, and we are about to separate for ever !"

" No ! No ! Never ! Long live Bertram our king !" shouted the excited crew, who could not yet comprehended the intention of their leader.

" Silence and hear me !" cried the leader. " You have said ye would *obey* me ! Am I yet your king ?"

" You are ! You are ! Long life to Bertram !"

" Listen ! There is now no safe place of rendezvous for you. The whole English navy is on the hunt for our band ! The only safety is to disperse ; the only alternative, to be hunted and harassed even unto death. It will be easy for you now to scatter among the islands with your wives and children, and unknown gradually to return to the world, where, if ye live prudently and well, your wealth will make you comfortable for life. I give you my share of all the treasure—I give you all the vessels, to bear you away, save the ship which ye have lately captured, and which now lies at anchor in yonder bay. Her I claim and the freedom of all my prisoners, for with them I return !"

" Oh, leave us not ! Be yet our king, and let us defy the world, and die as we have lived—bravely !" cried Consuelo, kneeling at the feet of the chief.

Loud was the shout of the whole crowd as they joined with Consuelo in the supplication.

" It may not be, my friends !" said Bertram, deeply affected by the appeal. " You know my will, you have sworn to obey me ; go, and so live, as in some measure to wash away the wrong of the past, in the good of the future !" Let the ship at once be fitted from my stores for a long voyage. Prepare everything to leave here, for short will be your rest, now that your homes are discovered. Hasten the preparations, and," he turned to the captains, " gentlemen, on you I depend for a just distribution among *my* people, for while my foot is yet on this shore I am your *king !*"

" Long live Bertram the noble and brave !" cried the people ; but there was a sadness in their cry which spoke but too plainly that the separation was not of their choice.

" Let my vessel be ready for sea by the morrow's sunrise, and then meet me once more upon this spot, my comrades ; and we will part for ever !"

Slowly and sadly the band turned away to their duties as the chief ceased.

" You see my power ! Do not I yield much in leaving them ?" asked young Edmiston of his father, as they dispersed.

" It is strange, exceedingly strange ! All this seems like a dream !" replied the father, musingly.

" Let us retire within and make our own preparations for the voyage," said the other, and in another moment the portico was vacant.

Again the morning's sun arose upon the pirate's home. The beautiful flag of the Sea King waved gaily out in a fresh breeze from the peak of the brig and also from the flag-staff before the house.

The men, women and children of the band were all assembled on the spot where they had stood before, and sadder yet than before was the gloom that pervaded each countenance which was turned toward their young chief, who stood, without his usual arms by his side, dressed not in his usual uniform, but in a plain seaman's attire, on the portico whence he had addressed them before.

" Consuelo !" said he to his favourite officer, " have all my orders been obeyed ? Is the ship ready for sea ? Has the wounded Captain been carefully conveyed on board his vessel ?"

Choked with emotion, the pirate could not answer ; he simply bowed an affirmative.

" It is well. Comrades and friends—we must part ! I have had you here assembled to bid you a final farewell ! Have I in all things dealt justly with ye since I have been your king."

" Ay, ay, in all things !" murmured some, while others in silence said even more, for tears and sighs are more expressive than words.

" Then am I contented. Consuelo, to you I give the last order of my power !" The pirate bowed, and awaited the command. " You have hands standing by to haul down the flag on board the brig ?"

" Your order has been obeyed !"

" Then lower the banner from yonder flag-staff, and as it descends so do I descend from my power."

The order was obeyed, and as the flag was lowered from the staff on shore, at the same time its counterpart on board the brig was taken in, while a mourning salute of minute-guns was fired from all the vessels. At the same moment, the mother, sister, and father of Edmiston, now no longer Bertram, appeared with Captain Danvers and the good Doctor, who appeared very differently now from when we last saw him fresh from the labours of his humane duties.

As they appeared, the deep silence which followed the lowering of the flag was broken by three long, thrilling cheers, for the relationship between their chief and these persons had been made known to them.

" Oh ! how much more musical are these sounds than the shouts of battle and the cries of the suffering !" said the mother, as she leaned upon the manly breast of her son, and wept in the fulness of her joy.

"Oh, yes," my mother—and yet I have revelled in the wild excitement of battle, have shouted with the mad joy of victory—but it is past, and for ever!   One moment forgive my absence, and then I will lead you to the boat which will take us to the ship!"

The youth relinquished his mother to her husband, and stepping down amongst his men bade them all farewell. Oh! many a tear coursed down their scarred and weather-beaten faces as he with kind words grasped their rough strong hands for the last time.

This last, and to him most painful duty over, he led his mother along the pathway to the boats at the landing. As they went, the little children threw flowers before them, and in sad silence the whole band followed them to the place of embarkation. Here they paused, all save those who were to go in the ship, which was strongly manned with the survivors of her old crew, and the English who had been saved from the battle.

The boats shoved off, and then one long, low cheer, not of joy—but expressive of sadness, mingled with love, was heard from the band on shore, who now felt that their brave and beloved chief was gone from them for ever.

While *he* waved his last farewell to them, tears gushed from his eyes, and he said

"They have vices, crimes, and faults, but they have at least one virtue, they have ever been *faithful!*"

In a few moments the party had reached the ship, then her anchor was hove up, her white sails loosed to the breeze, the American ensign hoisted at her peak, and piloted by him who had now assumed her command, she dashed out through the winding channel into the open sea like a steed just broken from the rein, impatient to improve its freedom.

Before the green trees of the island in their wake had sunk from sight in the distance, the crew of the ship saw the white sails of the piratical vessels specking the seas, as they left their village for ever, and then steered on different courses for other and more peaceful isles. The breeze was fresh and fair, and on like a bird belated in its homeward flight, the Mary dashed, with every stitch of canvass which her yards and spars would bear. Her course was shaped for England.

CHAPTER XX.

Forget ye the past,
And joy in the present,
For trouble at last,
Is buried for ever.

"FANNY, it's time that the Mary got into port ag'in! She's had a longer passage than Darlington generally makes! I do wish she'd come—I want to see Edmiston and his wife and our Lettie, as bad as ever I wanted to see daylight when I was close aboard a lee shore!" said Captain Bowline, as he sat enjoying a late breakfast.

"Haven't you seen her reported as arrived out, in the papers, yet?" asked the old lady.

"No, and I haven't thought to look afore. Just hand me the 'Journal,' and I'll take a squint at the shippin' list. Where's my specks gone to? I do believe that the confounded things have a knack of losin' themselves. When Fred was a little younger I could most generally account for 'em, for the young rascal had such a way with him. But, I say, Fanny, can't you find 'em?"

The old lady who had handed him the paper, now joined the jolly old Captain in the hunt for his spectacles, but as she had not her own upon her nose, she made a vain search.

"What are you looking for, mother?" asked a fine-looking young fellow, who had just entered the room, and whom the reader will recognise.

"For your father's specks, Freddy, my dear. Have you seen 'em?"

"Ha! ha!" laughed the lively youngster, as he seated himself at the breakfast table, opposite to his father.

"Have you been a hidin' 'em ag'in, you young lobster?" asked the father, a very little angry in his manner. The youth only laughed the harder. "Where *are* my specks, you Fred? I *order* you to give 'em to me:" now cried the father, with as cross an expression as his fat, good-humoured face could possible assume.

"I haven't them, father. They are stowed away atop of your head there, like a bowline-bridle on the booms."

"Well, so they are; but you needn't a made a laugh about it. It's decidedly disrespectful to the commanding officer," said the old Captain, more pacified upon finding his spectacles where he had placed them when he raised them above his eyes without removing them from his head. Then as he took up the paper, he added—"Now for the news. It is strange that I can't read without specks. Where's the shippin' list? Here's marriages and deaths and all that, but—I say, Fred!"

"Sir?"

"Lay down that ere knife and fork."

"Ay, ay, sir!"

"Take this ere paper and find me the shippin' list."

"Ay, ay, sir; here it is on the last column but one."

"Well, read it.   What a comfort it is to have a boy in one's old age who knows how to obey orders," and the old man chuckled as he looked upon the fine manly-looking fellow before him.

"What, the whole list, sir? Why, it's two columns long, and my coffee would be as cold as Mary Shield's heart before I got through. What do you want to find in it?"

"I want to see if there's any news of the Mary, you lazy lubber, you.   You ought to be put on half allowance, you had."

"The Mary!   Oh, yes, you mean Darlington's ship.   I'll look for that name with pleasure, for, as you know, I have quite a fancy for that name.   The Mary—let me see—yes, here's the Mary, spoken—lat. 29° 30', long. 79° 15', bound to Jamaica; but this is a brig, that ain't her.   Mary—Mary—let me see; no, there ain't no ship by that name reported in to-day's list."

"I hope they haven't met with pirates, or been wrecked," said Mrs. Bowline.

"Well, if they have met with pirates it would have to be something extra to catch the Mary, in the first place, and then if one should catch her, they might want to let her go ag'in, as the dog did the young hedge-hog, when he got a mouthful of quills for his breakfast.   The ship was well fitted for a fight, and both Darlington and Edmiston are Tartars when their dander's up."

"Well, if this ain't a go!   Now let people talk of romance.   If truth isn't stranger than fiction, then the small-pox adds to beauty," exclaimed young Bowline, jumping up from the table and capsizing the coffee-pot, while he kept his eyes fixed on the paper which he had been glancing over while his father was talking.

"Why, what on earth's the matter with the child?" exclaimed Mrs. Bowline; "there's the carpet ruined by that strong black coffee."

"Oh! never mind the carpet, mother. There's something besides coffee on the carpet.   Oh, such news!   How strange!"

"What is it, boy?   I do believe your head-gear has got out of order."

"Why, father, mother, just sit down and hear me read you this account from the paper.   Be quiet and let me read it all through before you jump up and break the things."

"Well, heave ahead, boy, and don't keep backing and filling there, and keeping us awaitin'."

"Well, I will, father. It is so strange, It is headed—'ROMANCE IN REAL LIFE.—We copy this morning the following article from a London journal, and were we not well acquainted with the general character of the paper for truth and correct information, we could not credit so strange a story. The account says—" By Captain

Danvers, who lately arrived in port, with a part of the crew of the line-of-battle ship Dromio, in the ship Mary, of Boston, commanded by Captain Edmiston, now, by the death of his late uncle, made Sir Edward Edmiston, we learn one of the strangest histories that has probably ever occurred. It appears that Sir Edward, when very young, was captured by a band of smugglers or pirates on the coast of America, whose chief adopted and reared him, and that until lately he has been among them, and is no other than the far-famed and long-feared KING OF THE SEA. By a series of most singular circumstances, his parents fell into his hands, and by some singular coincidences he became known to them, and on finding out his name and lineage, at once disbanded his crews and quitted for ever the profession which fate and circumstances, not his own will, had led him into. He had a most desperate combat with our naval forces about the time of this discovery, and although he conquered and could have destroyed them, he humanely spared them, and has now brought them home, and delivered himself to our government, confident of a free pardon, in consequence of the peculiar circumstances which left him amongst pirates in his childhood. We hope that one so noble, brave, and generous, will not be disappointed in the confidence which has induced him thus boldly to cast himself upon her Majesty's clemency. P.S.—Since writing the above, we are happy to learn that the Queen has not only granted a free pardon to Sir Edward, but expressed a deep admiration for his character, and desired him to be presented at court." ' "

"Can that be our little Eddy?" said Mrs. Bowline, as her son closed the paragraph.

"Pirate—coast of America—ship Mary—lord—what?" muttered Captain Bowline, quite stupified with surprise, and utterly unable to comprehend the story. At this moment a hasty ring of the door bell was heard. "There's somebody at the door, Freddy; now I do wonder if—— Give me that paper, Fred, before you go to the door; I won't believe that yarn about Edmiston though, if it is in the paper, for I do believe these editors do love to make up lies to bother old people and wimmen folks with."

The young man handed his father the paper and then went to the door, whence in a moment he returned, saying, "It's only the letter-man, father, and here's a letter directed to Captain John Bowline, Charlestown, Mass.; and it has a seal as big as one of my sweetheart's eyes, red wax and all sorts of funny figures in it. It's shaped like a shield, and has a mailed hand in one corner, which grasps a sword around which a serpent is twined, and then a lion in another corner, and two triangles in another, and a wild boar in the fourth; who can it be from, father?"

"Oh, don't bore me with your letter and seals, boy, don't you see I'm a readin'? You are my private secretary, why don't you read the letter and answer it, or do whatever you please, without bothering me. I suppose it's something about Edmiston's business; I wish he'd left somebody else to take care of his concerns, for it's a sin to nater to bother a man of my age and circumstances with business. Read the letter, yourself, and let me run over this yarn of the editor's."

"Ay, ay, sir!" responded the young hopeful, as he broke the armorial seal which had attracted his notice. He read a few lines in the letter, his face became agitated, his lips quivered, his eyes brightened, and he seemed as if about to "catch the crazy."

"What is the matter, Freddy, dear?" inquired his anxious mother.

Fred read a few more lines, then deliberately kicked the break-fast-table over—kissed his mother, ran foul of his father's gouty feet, which had received a fair share of the contents of the coffee-ot, which was too hot to be agreeable for a foot-bath, and by sundry strange and singular antics, now thoroughly convinced his parents that his head-gear was out of order.

"Avast there, you young lubber! steer clear of my toes; what on earth do ye mean?—speak, or, by thunder, I'll knock you down !" shouted Captain Bowline, as he rubbed his damaged underpin.

"Oh, Freddy, dear, what *is* the matter? Why do you carry on so? I do believe the poor child has gone stark starin' mad!" ex-claimed Mrs. Bowline, at the same time retreating out of harm's way into the farthest corner of the room, where, with uplifted hands and wondering eyes, she stood and saw the young man dance a hornpipe over the broken dishes which strewed her carpet.

But his excitement, like the bursting of a corked beer bottle, worked off its own cure, and becoming a little calmer, he rapidly run off the following broken but explanatory sentences : "Oh, father—mother! it's a letter from England—from Captain Edmis-ton—and it *is* little Edward that the paper tells about, and he *is* a noble; and, oh, thunder and poppies! wait till I get breath, and I'll tell you the rest !" and the young man sunk into a chair with such decided symptoms of choking, that his kind mother, fancying that he had got a fish-bone in his throat, rushed to his side, and administered sundry and many heavy thumps upon his back, calling upon her dear child "to spit it out !"

The father, who now began to comprehend the case, and was impatient for a full explanation, cried, " Let the youngster alone, Fanny, and let the boy read us the letter. Come, heave ahead, Fred, and let us know what's to pay !"

"Ay, ay, sir," responded the son, more calmly, and then read as follows :—" 'Dear Bowline—I am overjoyed to acquaint you that I have found my long-lost son, and that he is now with me in London, has succeeded to the title and estates of his grandfather, Sir Lancelot Edmiston, and is as noble a specimen of manhood as a fond father could wish or hope for. It would be too long a story in a letter to attempt to tell how, where, and when I found him; but I soon shall be alongside of you, and then you shall have full explanations. My wife is well and happy—oh! I cannot say how happy! Lettie has not only found a brother, but—I'll leave you to guess what else she has found to add to her happiness. I think we shall come over in the next steamer, for I have sold the Mary; and poor Darlington is on his beam-ends with injuries received in a desperate battle with pirates, in the Mozambique Channel; but he'll be able to come over with us. I shall quit the mercantile business now for ever, and retire to the quietude of private life, for I have had enough of strife, and excitement, and change, to satisfy even my restless nature.

"'I wish you to keep your conversation-hatches battened down in regard to *all* of this news, for I do not wish my son to be *lionized,* nor does he wish to be known in America as any other than the son of a republican. You must be very careful to keep your lips closed about the matter, for *one whisper* set afloat on the expansive air of your town, would soon spread into a yarn longer than a 74's maintop-bowline. I do believe that the place is peculiarly adapted for hearing, carrying, and making news. But returning to my return. If you will have a carriage at the wharf when the Acadia comes over on her next trip, you'll be likely to find a load for it; and if Providence spares us, you will receive a hearty grasp from the hand of,

Yours ever faithfully,   EDMISTON.

"'P. S. Do be careful to keep the news I have told you quiet, for I dread the idea of being lionized, and my boy won't stay three hours in your place if any attempt is made to lionize or be-lord him. Farewell till we meet, and give the kindest remembrances of all to your lady, &c., &c.   S. E.'"

"Is that all, Fred?" asked Bowline, raising the spectacles from his nose, and carefully wiping them with his red bandanna.

"Yes, sir, every word."

"Let me read it!"

"Ay, ay, sir!" and the son handed him the letter.

Slowly and carefully did the old gentleman peruse the letter, and then, without saying a word, handed it to his wife, who, likewise, having cleaned the dust from her spectacles, also read it.

"Well, I do declare!" was her simple but exceedingly expressive remark, as she finished its perusal.

"What are you overhauling in your mind's locker, Fred, that keeps you in such a brown study?" asked the father, noticing the uncommon quiet of the former, as he sat apparently regarding the wreck of the breakfast-table.

"I was wondering what it could be that Captain Edmiston says that Lettie has found besides her brother, to make her happy!"

"Yes, I do wonder!" added the mother.

"Why, a good husband, to be sure! That's the very thing to make a girl of her age happy!"

"So it is, father, and that's what she has found!'

"But who *would* ha' thought it?" said Mrs. Bowline, and then, as her eye rested upon her half-ruined carpet, she added, "Oh! Freddy, do see how naughty you have acted!"

"Well, mother, I couldn't help it, as the cow remarked with her 'speaking eyes,' to the dairy-maid, after kicking over the milk-pail!"

"Well, well, it's done, and it can't be helped. Call Lizzy, and let her clear away the wreck!" said the old gentleman, who was too happy to be angry.

*   *   *   *   *

It was precisely one month and three days after the occurrence of the scene above described, that the same room was occupied by nine instead of three people, as before.

The reader will recognise in them Captain Edmiston and his happy wife, Sir Edward Edmiston, Doctor Blount Hazlewood and his wife, and Captain Darlington, who was still pale and feeble. Of course the Bowlines were there, and these completed as happy a party as ever formed a circle around a cheerful table.

The secret had been carefully kept by the Bowlines, and as neither the Bostonians nor Charlestown people knew that a *real* nobleman had honored their respective cities with a visit, he was allowed to pass about unnoticed, without more attention than any other well-dressed and decently-behaved individual would have received. He was not invited to any public dinners, the theatres sent him no complimentary invitations (which would have drawn them such full houses had he been known), nor was the "old Faneuil" opened to give him a ball.

Their visit to the Bowlines was indeed a happy one, for there they were received as friends should be, with warm and open hearts, without the cold and ceremonious etiquette which but too often makes even civility painfully disagreeable. They were received as friends should receive friends, for the real pleasure of long and fondly-cherished associations, and for the real merit of themselves, not their rank or fortune.

Oh! that there was more of that true republican spirit in the country which recognises no aristocracy but that of mind, virtue, and merit; which makes the title of MAN more respectable than the name which *title* can give; which yields to merit the honour which fortune cannot command!

The separation between the Bowline family and the Edmistons was rendered far less sad, by a promise of a speedy visit from the former, who, as the steamer that bore them homeward backed out of the East Boston dock, waved many a fond adieu, wishing them as we wish you, reader, all manner of happiness and good fortune till we meet again, which we may hope for, wind and weather permitting.

THE END

www.ingramcontent.com/pod-product-compliance
Lightning Source LLC
Chambersburg PA
CBHW081305200626
46813CB00018B/3217